The Orphan King

· BOOK ONE ·
MERLIN'S IMMORTALS

Sigmund Brouwer

WATERB
PRE

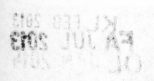

THE ORPHAN KING
PUBLISHED BY WATERBROOK PRESS
12265 Oracle Boulevard, Suite 200
Colorado Springs, Colorado 80921

The characters and events in this book are fictional, and any resemblance to actual persons or events is coincidental.

ISBN 978-1-4000-7154-8
ISBN 978-0-307-73065-7 (electronic)

Cover design by Mark Ford

Published in the United States by WaterBrook Multnomah, an imprint of the Crown Publishing Group, a division of Random House Inc., New York.

WATERBROOK and its deer colophon are registered trademarks of Random House Inc.

Library of Congress Cataloging-in-Publication Data
Brouwer, Sigmund, 1959–
   The orphan king : a novel / Sigmund Brouwer.—1st ed.
      p. cm.
   ISBN 978-1-4000-7154-8 (alk. paper)—ISBN 978-0-307-73065-7 (electronic)
   1. Druids and Druidism—Fiction. I. Title.
   PS3552.R6825O77 2012
   813'.54—dc23

                              2012007306

Printed in the United States of America
2012—First Edition

10 9 8 7 6 5 4 3 2 1

Author's Note

Twenty years and almost as many novels have passed since I wrote this sentence: "Since dawn, three ropes had hung black against the rising sun."

I can remember where I was sitting as I began with those words, the time of day, the light of the sun as it fell across the table where I sat, and how it seemed as if the events that followed didn't belong to me, and that instead I had been given a chance to observe and relay the unfolding of a story.

While some of the events in *The Orphan King* may be familiar to readers of *Magnus* or *Wings of Dawn*, much of that original story from twenty years earlier remained untold. I'm grateful with *The Orphan King* to have the chance to return and begin exploring all that happened in the intricate battle of two great forces, each facing the necessity to remain hidden from the society around it.

If you traveled with Thomas on his quest all those years ago when I first did, I hope you enjoy, as I have, the chance to join him again with fresh eyes and new perspectives.

Enter a medieval world of love and chivalry,
of ancient secrets,
an evil conspiracy, noble knights,
and a mysterious castle called
Magnus…

SPRING, NORTHERN ENGLAND — AD 1312

Amidst the shouting and haggling in the crowded and filthy market square, two women appeared to be examining the quality of spun wool.

Neither was a woman.

And neither cared about the wool.

The men in dresses and shawls and coarse wigs beneath bonnets had chosen this disguise because they could not risk the chance of anyone linking the two of them. It was a minuscule risk, that perhaps one day someone might note first one had gone into a church—or any other meeting place—and then the other. Yet even the slightest risk was too much.

They each held one end of the spun wool and leaned in close so nobody could overhear a single word.

"You know what the planets and stars tell us about tomorrow morning, don't you?" the older man said.

"Of course," the younger answered. "I wonder why we don't use events like this to our advantage. Think of the power it would give us, making it appear that we control the heavens."

"That would require revealing that we exist."

The second man sighed. "Yes. Over the years you've made it very clear that the true power is exerting control without letting the person controlled know of it."

"A thousand years now. Shouldn't that be—"

"Yes, yes." The younger man was prone to impatience and prone to showing it. "A thousand years hidden among them. Shouldn't that be enough indication of the wisdom of our strategy? Is that what you were going to say?"

They paused as a couple of women stepped too close, then resumed as soon as those women had moved on again.

"When I pass on my mantle to you," the older one said, "and when you choose someone to take your place, you'll hear yourself repeating much of what I've said. Now think. It is significant that tomorrow morning was chosen for the hanging. Why?"

There was a long pause. The second man picked at some bugs in the wool as he thought it through. Then he exclaimed, "The knight is bait!"

"This is why you have been chosen as my successor. You see and understand what others cannot. Yes. I'm sure they want to use the knight to draw him out. Think again. How can we use that to our advantage?"

The younger man didn't hesitate. "For years, we have been searching for him too. When we find him, we will find what they have stolen from us and given to him."

"And how is this a danger to us?"

"If they find him and use him, it could lead them to what was stolen from us and given to him."

"Every sword has two edges. We must keep Magnus at all costs. Losing it is the edge of the sword that can wound us. For them, the reward of regaining Magnus puts them in danger from the other edge of the sword. If the knight truly is bait, as we suspect, they must expose themselves as they try to win him to their side. More importantly, if the knight is bait and draws him out, we will have a chance to take him for ourselves."

"All these years. He is into manhood now."

"Yes, I expect he will be a formidable opponent. But once he reveals himself, we can use the structure of law to hunt him."

"And kill him?" the younger asked.

"Unless he will serve us instead. What he possesses is a great prize."

"To reach him also means exposing ourselves," the younger one said with a degree of satisfaction, expecting to be praised for this brilliant observation.

"I hope I don't die soon," the older man said with mild irony.

"What do you mean by that?"

"Because I have so much left to teach you. If we know the knight is bait, don't you think it's wise to make sure we have our own bait?"

"I don't understand."

Still looking down at the spun wool, the older man said, "The knight is not the only one on the gallows tomorrow."

The younger man's eyes opened in surprise, then he blinked in comprehension. "So we cannot lose," he said.

"No," the older one said. "We are Druids. We never lose."

TWO

As bells rang for *none,* the church service three hours past midday, Thomas should have been toiling in the gardens of the abbey and knew that he risked a flogging if he were caught. But compared to the actions he was considering, abandoning the garden was a minor crime not worth giving a second thought.

Conscious, though, that it would be much better for his absence not to be noticed, Thomas moved quickly. He glanced back to see if he'd been followed and saw only the cold stone walls of the abbey hall blurred by trees. The valley that contained the abbey was narrow and compressed, more rock and stunted trees on the slopes than sweet grass and sheep—probably the reason it had been donated to the mother abbey long ago by an earl determined to buy his way into heaven.

The mother abbey at Rievaulx, just outside of Helmsley, was part of the large order of Cistercian monks and had always accepted such gifts. With this one, Rievaulx had quickly established an outpost designed to earn more money for the church. Time had proven the land too poor, however, and barely worth the investment of abbey hall, library, and living quarters made from stone quarried directly from the nearby hills.

Thomas moved quickly through an exposed patch of hillside into the trees near the tiny river that wound past the abbey. Years of avoiding the harsh monks had taught him secret ways through the old abbey, hidden paths on the abbey grounds, and every deer trail in the surrounding hills. He had been forced to learn how to move quietly. At times he would approach a seemingly solid stand of brush, then slip sideways into an invisible opening among the jagged branches and later reappear farther down the hill.

His familiarity with the terrain, however, did not make him less cautious. He shuddered at the consequences of allowing the monks to discover what he had hidden from them all these years.

Several bends upstream from the abbey hall, comfortably shaded by large oaks, stood a jumble of rocks and boulders, some as large as a peasant's hut. Among them, a freak of nature had created a dry, cool cave, its narrow entrance concealed by jutting slabs of granite and bushes rising from softer ground below.

Thomas circled it once. Then he slipped into a crevice and surveyed the area.

"Count to one thousand," echoed the instructions that had been given to him time and again. *"Watch carefully for movement and count to one thousand. Let no person ever discover this place."*

Thomas settled into the comforting hum of forest noises, alert for any sign of intruders, and pondered the day.

First, he would need the power of knowledge hidden within the cave. Then time to assemble that power. Thomas half smiled. *So much waiting inside among the books...*

Enough time had passed. He circled slowly once more, remembering, as he did every time, the love Sarah had given him along with the instructions.

"Never, never speak of the existence of the books. Always, always, be sure beyond doubt no person sees you slip into the cave. The books have the power of knowledge beyond price. Take from them, and never, never speak of their existence."

When Thomas stepped in the coolness of the cave, sadness overwhelmed him with the darkness. It never failed to remind him of his mother and how badly he missed her and the secrets she'd made him keep, secrets for keeping both of them safe.

He knew it was his imagination, but as always, he believed he could hear, somewhere in the darkness, how she'd whispered on her deathbed the startling revelations that he'd had to hold deep inside.

"Thomas, there is so much I wanted to tell you when you were older. I believed this was just another fever, but now I cannot deny that I will be gone before the hour. Thomas, I am your mother and love you as much as any mother has loved any son. I took you and fled from evil men to hide from them here, men who pretend one thing during the light of day and another at night, men who believe in human sacrifices. My greatest fear is that someday they would find us and make of us a sacrifice beneath a full moon, burning us alive in baskets hanging from an oak tree in the same manner that they killed your father and your older brother and older sister, when they took the kingdom from our family. Thomas, pretend, always, that I was your nursemaid, as I pretended to you all these years. My prayer was to watch you grow into a man and become one of us, one of the Immortals. You will help us destroy the circle of evil."

In her final minutes he wept in her arms, trying to comprehend her words, begging her to sit up and sing to him again. She'd clutched his wrists with a supernatural strength, as if she were clinging to life itself. Then came a single moment of fierceness and clarity as she'd found the energy, just before collapsing with a final breath, to make him swear that he would someday understand and destroy the evil that had sent them fleeing.

Thomas knelt as he always did when entering the cave. Not in prayer, but in honor of her memory. And he spoke into the emptiness, as he always did upon kneeling. "I will never forget you. I will never forget the sacrifices you made for me. I will never forget my vow to you upon your deathbed. I will protect with my life what you have given me, and I will use it as you have directed."

Saying it, however, he felt a shiver of fear. And hated himself for it.

Thomas felt like a knight in a legend who proudly told the king he would slay a dragon. Easy to promise far, far from a fire-breathing monster. But nearing the dragon's lair, as the smell of sulphur grew stronger and the sound of shifting scales came from the gloom ahead, few were the men whose bowels wouldn't loosen in fear. Few were the men who would lift a sword and plunge forward.

For Thomas, his time was nearly upon him, and he was discovering that he wasn't among the few whose bravery could overcome the roar of the dragon. He wanted to be a boy again, when a simple caress of Sarah's fingers across his cheek and a gentle song were all that was needed to ease the tremblings of nightmares.

He stood motionless, steadying his breathing until his eyes adjusted to the gloom. He waited another fifteen minutes. Then he moved forward to the shaft of sunlight that fell through a large crack where one slab leaned crookedly against another.

With little hesitation, he pulled aside a rotting piece of tree that looked as if it had grown into the rock. Thomas dragged out a chest as high as his knees and as wide as a cart. He opened the lid, reached inside, and gently lifted out a leather-bound book the size of a small tabletop.

He searched page after page, carefully turning and setting down each leaf of ancient paper before scanning the words.

Nearly an hour later, he grunted with satisfaction. His plans were sound. If he had the courage, it was possible to succeed in a seemingly impossible task.

Magnus could be his. An orphan boy could claim the power and authority of a near king. And with that power, he could begin the hunt that he'd vowed to his mother.

But only if he had the courage. Nothing in his life had tested him, proven to him that he was capable of slaying a dragon. He fought his shiver of fear and fought the impulse of self-hatred and, kneeling again, repeated his vows.

"I will never forget you. I will never forget the sacrifices you made for me. I will never forget my vow to you upon your deathbed. I will protect with my life what you have given me, and I will use it as you have directed."

Even so, he couldn't help but wonder if it was a lie.

Without hurry, he returned the book to the chest, then the chest into its spot in the stone, then the lumber in front of the chest. There were other bundles, the contents very familiar to him, that he scooped into his arms. Finally, he was ready to take them and hide them outside the cave.

To be absolutely certain it was safe, he silently counted to one thousand at the entrance of the ruins before edging back into the forest with the intent to move the bundles to a safe place well away from the abbey. Only then would he return to his menial labor in the garden.

And, as always when leaving the cave, he wondered about his mother's last words.

Who were the Immortals?

The monks—only four of them because the abbey was so small and insignificant—finished their evening meal, and Thomas began to clear away the pots and greasy plates. The monks were in no hurry to push back from the table. Their goblets of mead—a wine of fermented honey and water—were only half-empty, and there was another full jug in front of them to finish at their leisure.

If it remained a typical night, they would sit at the table for at least another hour, drinking and belching and picking their teeth. If it remained a typical night, as Thomas had been planning, he'd take advantage of this and flee the abbey.

If he could find the courage.

Now well past the age of an apprentice, Thomas had been raised in this abbey since a boy. He'd known no other life except one that forced work upon him from before the rise of the sun to long after the first candles had been lit. Until he discovered a letter from the mother abbey a few months earlier, it had never occurred to him to resent the tasks put upon him. Repeatedly the monks had told him that if it weren't for their generosity in allowing him to stay at the abbey, he'd be homeless and wandering the countryside like any other orphan. He'd believed it. Until finding the letter in an obscure part of the abbey's archives.

Yet during the years of believing he must depend on the charity of these men—long, long before finding the letter—he'd come to loathe their gluttony. Each meal he watched them gorge themselves to the point of illness, enjoying fattened geese and grain-fed ducks and chicken. In the mornings, when women came to the gate to beg for alms for the dirty and rail-thin children clinging to their hands, the monks would send them away, quoting biblical verses from Proverbs about the need for industry and self-sufficiency, casting blame on the mothers for their apparent laziness. This, even though the abbey had been founded with permission from the king on the agreement that a percentage of the abbey's income be dedicated to the poor.

Everything in his mind told Thomas this was the night he must flee and never return.

He needed courage, because as Thomas was reluctant to admit to himself, a man is more often driven by the heart than the mind.

Over the past week, he'd used his mind and all his other resources to make the plans that, in the cool silence of the cave where he often hid from the monks, seemed to have no flaw. In the world of his dreams, he could picture himself as the hero, overcoming every obstacle set in his path. In those dreams, fear did not exist. In those dreams, matters of the mind triumphed over matters of the heart. In those dreams, intellect conquered emotion.

Outside the cave, however, was the real world of cold and hunger, of sheriffs and soldiers armed with crossbows and swords, of dark forests and narrow roads where every corner might hide roaming bandits eager to prey upon the weak. Of a castle with impregnable defenses.

Beneath the trees and the rustling leaves just outside the sanctuary of the cave, Thomas would feel the fear that did not exist inside the cave, knowing those all-too-real dangers should force him to reconsider the boldness of the plans. Even so, it was more than a lack of courage that gave him doubts.

He was an orphan. When Sarah had died, he had lost the last of his family. He had only memories of her, and questions about the father and the older brother and sister who had been taken from him before there could be memories. Pitiful as the children were who clung to their mothers outside the gates, they had something Thomas did not. A true sense of belonging.

Thomas had a shadow of this feeling, enough to identify the source of what made him ache during his loneliest moments. Inside the abbey, despite the abuse heaped upon him, Thomas was still part of a group, with rituals and the familiarity of what to expect each day. He had a bed, miserable as the straw ticking was, and a room of his own.

This was a comfort of sorts, enough to hint at what it might feel like to be part of a real family, loved and secure. As it was, he did belong to this group, even if the men in this group were arrogant and unkind and treated him with more disdain than they did the livestock. It was one thing to be lonely—he could endure this because he had no choice. It was another thing to be alone.

Could he find the courage to make the choice to become alone?

To flee the abbey would not only force him to risk his life on a plan that seemed to contain too many obstacles to succeed, but it would also cast him into the unknown, out into the world where he would not have even the certainty of knowing where he would rest each night. Compared to that, the occasional beating from Prior Jack did not seem like such a poor bargain.

The truth was simple. He was more afraid of being alone than of failing. The combination of the two fears was almost overwhelming.

Thomas wasn't certain he could find the courage to flee the abbey, even after he'd learned through that letter about the injustice of his imprisonment among the monks.

If his courage failed him, he would regret it until he died. For at dawn the next day, a certain knight would be executed by hanging. And this was the man that destiny had promised him.

Which led Thomas to another question.

Did he have the courage to turn his back on destiny?

THREE

I t did not remain a typical evening.

As Thomas reached to take the empty plate in front of Prior Jack, the fat man grabbed the collar of Thomas's tunic and yanked Thomas downward with such unexpected violence that his face slammed into a pile of chicken bones beside Prior Jack's plate.

"I did not see you in the garden today," Prior Jack said with a chilling calmness.

At impact with the table, one of the discarded chicken bones had snapped on the point of his jaw, and Thomas felt a sharp pain where the jagged edge cut through his skin. He blinked against the pain, the rough wood of the table a blur beneath his eyes.

"Jack, I doubt that kind of intimidation is needed," came the voice of an older monk, Philip.

"He's a fully grown man," Jack answered in the permanent wheeze that resulted from his gross fatness, a state that also forced him to waddle sideways through most of the abbey's narrower doorways. "He needs to be taught again and again that his size doesn't matter when it comes to disobeying us. I believe he should be flogged."

Thomas did not move. He could not move. Prior Jack was massive. Thomas was in an unbalanced position, something that a bully like Prior Jack undoubtedly knew. By the tone of the man's voice, Thomas could picture Prior Jack's eyes as pinpoints of black hatred almost hidden in rolls of flesh.

Once, on a sweltering summer day, Thomas had heard splashing in the pond behind the abbey. He'd crept closer and seen Prior Jack waist-deep in the water. So wide and blubbery were the rolls of stark white fat that Thomas could barely recognize the shape of a man beneath the boulder-shaped head.

Not that fatness was unfashionable. On the contrary; it was a status symbol. Only the rich could afford it. Most peasants suffered from continuous hunger and considered themselves fortunate each day to eat more than a bowl of thin cabbage soup and some slices of black wholemeal bread, never with butter. Yet Prior Jack took advantage of the distance of Harland Moor Abbey from the mother abbey, becoming a tyrant in relentless pursuit of his gluttony.

"Our soil is poor enough as it is," Prior Jack explained to the others, keeping Thomas's head firmly pinned against the chicken bones. Thomas felt warmth on his chin. His own blood. "If he continues to neglect the garden, fall harvest might only last until January."

Yes, Thomas thought, *because the monks eat five meals a day.*

"More to the point," Prior Jack said, "is the question of where Thomas goes. I demand an answer."

It is not the mind that drives a man, but emotion. For all his worry about whether he'd find the courage to flee, in the end it was anger that tipped Thomas toward his own destiny.

He'd been humiliated by these men daily, but this time, the snapping of the chicken bones snapped something inside him. Nobody deserved to be stooped over a table, face pressed into the discards of another man's meal.

"Prior Jack," Thomas said through gritted teeth as he reached into his shirt with his right hand. "You are a fat, obscene pig." Thomas pulled his hand free. "If you don't let go, this knife will slice lard off you in strips."

He jabbed the blade into the fat man's side, knowing it pierced skin and the first layer of fat.

Prior Jack yelped and let go.

Thomas straightened and pulled his knife free from Prior Jack. The tip ran red with blood. Thomas wiped the blade against his sleeve and pointed the knife at Prior Jack's face.

"Any move at all from any of you," Thomas said, "and I stab out his eyes."

He felt exultant. Perhaps that had been his reluctance to flee—not a lack of courage but the need to be openly defiant. Slipping out in the night while the monks were drunk would have shown his fear of them. But to threaten these bullies at knifepoint was an act of rebellion that would not allow turning back. Effectively, he'd just become an outlaw. Escape was not an option; it was a necessity.

He was ready; he was strong.

Prior Jack rattled a gasp from his overworked lungs. "How dare you threaten me! I am a man of God!"

Thomas took a deep breath and spoke words that erupted from years of supplication to these loathsome men.

"You? A man of God? First convince me that God exists. Then convince me you're a man, not a spineless pig of jelly. And finally, if God does exist, prove to me that you actually follow Him instead of preaching one thing and doing another."

The fat monk's cheeks bulged in horror. How astounding it must have seemed; for years Thomas had formed his defiance through simple silence.

This horror added to Thomas's sense of freedom. Like steel revealed behind a falling cloth, it was if he'd suddenly discovered he was no longer a scrawny boy but that his corded muscles had taken him into manhood. If there was irony in this rebellion, it was that all the unending work forced upon him had built those muscles.

The knife in his right hand did not waver.

Prior Jack dropped his voice to an unusual strained wheeze. "Put the knife away. Immediate penitence may spare your soul after such blasphemy. Or these men will stop you immediately."

Dust danced between them, red and blue in the light beams from a stained-glass window on the west side of the corridor. It reminded Thomas that the sun was at a sharp angle. Eventide would be upon him soon.

His plan must work. But first he must get past this detestable bully and the three other monks. Would he actually murder to obtain his freedom?

The others stared at him, their shaved heads faintly pink.

"The boy has lost his mind," Prior Jack whined to them. "He is threatening to kill me. Do something!"

Monk Walter, gaunt and gray, frowned. "Put the knife down, boy. Now. And you will only be whipped as punishment. If not, you will lose your hand."

Thomas knew that was no idle threat. Peasants *had* had their hands cut off for simple crimes like theft. To threaten members of the clergy was unimaginable.

"Tonight," Thomas said calmly instead of dropping the knife, "is the night you set me free from this hole that is hell on earth. Furthermore, you will send me on my way with provisions for a week and also three years' wages."

"Impertinent dog," squeaked Monk Philip. Tiny and shrunken, he quickly looked to the others for approval. "You owe us the best years of your life. Few abbeys in this country would have taken in scum like you and raised you as we did."

"As a slave?" Thomas countered. He lifted his knife higher, and they kept their distance. "Since I was old enough to lift a hoe, you sent me to the garden. When I cried because of raw blisters, you cuffed me on the head and withheld my food. Your filth—dirty, stinking clothing and the slop of your meals—I've cleaned every day for seven years. In the winter, I chopped wood in the mornings while you slept indoors, too cheap to give me even a shawl for my blue shoulders."

Monk Frederick rose on his toes and pointed at Thomas. His greasy face turned red with indignation. "We could have thrown you to the wolves!"

Thomas spat at their feet. "Listen to me, you old, feeble men." He felt a surge of hot joy. The moment was right; he knew without doubt. The hesitation that had filled him with agony had disappeared.

"Listen," Thomas repeated, ready to reveal he'd found the letter in the archives, the one that Sarah promised was there. "You did not take me in as charity. You took me in because the prior at Rievaulx ordered that you care for me and the nurse."

Even now, Thomas had to pretend Sarah had been nothing more than that, a nursemaid. He continued the fiction, fully aware of the price Sarah paid to keep them hidden. "The prior did so because my parents were not peasants as you have tried to lead me to believe. My father was a mason, a builder of churches, and left behind enough money to pay for my education."

No, he'd been a man sacrificed beneath a full moon. By men that Thomas would hunt and destroy.

Thomas continued. "Yet you took advantage of the distance from the abbey at Rievaulx, and instead of providing an education, you used me as a slave."

Monk Philip glanced wildly at the other three. "He cannot know that," he sputtered.

"No?" Thomas's voice grew ominous. As he spoke, he saw by the reactions of the monks how much strength he had carefully hidden from them, and to his surprise, from himself. Thomas let his tone grow cold, and he spoke quietly enough to make them strain for every savage word. "The letters you leave carelessly about speak plainly to me. I've read every report—every false report—that you have sent to the prior at Rievaulx, including the first one, which affirms that you are doing the Christian duty to me that you were charged to do. Bah!" Thomas made his contempt plain. "I wish I was half as content as you have made him believe."

Monk Walter shook his head. "You cannot read. That is a magic, a gift the clergy give to very few."

Thomas ignored him. "Furthermore, I have written in clear Latin a long letter that details the history of this abbey over the last years. I have also transcribed the letter into French, with that copy reserved for the Earl of York."

"Thomas writes too?" gasped Monk Philip. "Latin *and* French?"

"These letters are in the hands of a friend in the village. Unless I appear tonight to ask for them back, he will deliver them to the mother abbey. All of you will be defrocked and sent penniless among the same peasants you have robbed for years."

"It's a bluff," Prior Jack declared. "If we all move at once, we can lay hold of him and deliver him to the sheriff—for hanging."

Time ebbed heartbeat by heartbeat in the stillness of the abbey.

Thomas held up his hand, and the sudden motion checked any rash action. "Monk Frederick. Your accounting of the wool taken from the sheep that I guarded night after night. Will it bear close scrutiny when the prior at Rievaulx sends men to examine the records? Or will they discover you have been keeping one bag of wool for every ten sold and turning the profit into gold for yourself?"

Frederick's face grew white.

"Don't worry," Thomas said. "The strongbox you have hidden in the hollow of a tree behind the pond is safe. But empty of your gold. That has been given to my friend in the village as payment to hold my letters, a payment that will be distributed among the poor whom you have failed so badly to comfort."

The other monks swiveled their heads to stare at Frederick.

"I see," Thomas said. "The gold was a secret."

A growl from Prior Jack proved the statement true.

"Prior Jack," Thomas snorted. "Tending to your dishes after each meal made my task very easy. The letter also details the food you consume in a single month. I'm sure the prior at Rievaulx will be disappointed to discover that you slobber down nearly four hundred eggs from full moon to full moon. Over fifty pounds of flour. Three lambs. And a side of beef. It will explain, of course, why this abbey has not made a harvest contribution to the mother abbey in five years."

Prior Jack's cheeks wobbled with rage.

"Tut, tut," Thomas cautioned. "Anger, like work, may strain your heart."

"Enough," Monk Walter said.

"Enough? Is it because you dread to hear what that letter reports of you?"

The lines of Monk Walter's face drew tight. "You shall get the provisions you demand."

"This means, I take it, that your fellow monks don't know *your* secret vice?"

"You will also receive three years' wages," Monk Walter said.

"He's a male witch," Thomas announced to the other three. "A practicing warlock. Potions, magic chanting, and the sacrifice of animals at midnight."

The other three monks recoiled from Monk Walter.

"Oh, don't worry," Thomas said. "He's quite harmless. I've heard him sobbing into his pillow from failure more times than I care to recall."

In the renewed silence, they could only stare at one another. Four monks in shabby brown. A full-grown boy with enough calm hatred to give him strength.

Thomas was the first to break the silence. "I will take my wages in silver or gold. Have it here before the sun is down, along with the provisions. Or I shall demand *four* years' wages instead."

They hesitated.

"Go on," Thomas said. "I'll keep my word and have the letters returned when I have escaped safely."

They rose from the table and scurried as he'd commanded; even before rounding the corner of the hall, they'd already begun heated arguing and accusations.

Shortly after, the last rays of sun warmed the stained glass as Monk Walter and Monk Philip strode back to Thomas in the dining hall.

Monk Walter held out an oily leather bag. "Cheese, bread, and meat," he said. "Enough to last you ten days."

Monk Philip tossed Thomas a much smaller sack. "Count it," he said. "Two years in silver. Another year in gold."

Thomas regarded them steadily. Where was the fear with which they had departed barely a half-hour earlier? Why the gleam of triumph behind Monk Walter's eyes?

"Thank you," Thomas said as the comforting weight of both sacks dragged on his arms. Yet he did not leave. An unease he could not explain filled him.

"Go on, boy," Monk Walter sneered in the gathering darkness of the hall.

Still Thomas waited. Unsure.

Monk Philip gazed at the rough stones beneath his feet. "In the letter," he mumbled, "what have you to tell the prior at Rievaulx about me?"

Thomas suddenly felt pity. The tiny man's shoulders were bowed with weariness and guilt.

"Nothing to damn you," he said gently. "Nothing to praise you. As if you merely stood aside all these years."

"You show uncanny wisdom for a boy," Monk Philip choked out, his head still low. When he straightened, he made no effort to hide tears. "Perhaps that is the worst of all, not to make a choice between good or evil. I'm old now. I can barely hear, yet the slightest noise wakens me from troubled sleep. My bones are brittle and I'm afraid of falling, even from the steps to the chapel. The terrifying blackness of death is too soon ahead of me, and all I am to the God who waits is an empty man who has only pretended to be in His service."

"Quit your blathering," Monk Walter said between clenched teeth. "Send the boy on his way. Now!"

Monk Philip clamped his jaw as if coming to a decision. "Not to his death. Nor shall I go meet God without attempting some good." He drew a lungful of air. "Thomas, leave alone the—"

Monk Walter crashed a fist into the tiny man's mouth. The blow drove Monk Philip's head into a square stone that jutted from the wall. He collapsed to his knees without a moan. He smiled once at Thomas, struggled to speak, then toppled to the floor and did not move.

Thomas felt a chill. What had Philip been trying to say?

"Spawn of the devil," Monk Walter hissed at Thomas. "Your soul will roast in hell."

Thomas said nothing and rested the bag of food on his shoulder. He took half a step away, then turned to deliver a promise.

"Monk Walter," he began with quiet deadliness, guessing suddenly the reason for Philip's death, "if indeed there is such a place as hell, your soul will be there much sooner than mine."

Thomas left the hall as silently as his shadow. He paused outside until the noises inside told him that the three remaining monks were struggling with Monk Philip's body. Then, to fulfill his parting promise, Thomas slipped to the rear of the abbey into the cool storage room dug below the kitchen.

He departed shortly after into the darkness, climbing the valley hills with one fewer sack than he had planned.

FOUR

All stared at the soon-to-be-dead.

Since dawn, three ropes had hung black against the rising sun. Enough time had passed for a crowd to arrive and develop a restless holiday mood, jeering when the prisoners were finally hauled in a wagon to the gallows.

"Hear ye, hear ye, all gathered here today." The caller, short and dumpy with middle age, made no effort to hide the boredom in his voice.

His words had little effect on the hundred people crowded in front of the crude wooden gallows. Each person had eyes only for the soon-to-be-dead.

"Get on with your blathering, you old fool!" The shout came from a woman with a hungry face near the back of the crowd. A skinny child held her hand.

The man scratched at a flea beneath his dirty shirt and ignored her.

"This punishment has been ordered by the sheriff under authority of the Earl of York," he continued in a listless tone. "The crimes to be punished are as follows." He unrolled a scroll and held it in front of him at arm's length.

"Andrew, you dimwit! We all know you can't read. Don't be putting on airs for the likes of us." This from a fat man with jowls that shook as he yelled.

The crowd hooted with appreciation even though none of them, including the speaker, realized the scroll was upside down. They grew quiet again.

And all stared at the soon-to-be-dead.

Six burly soldiers stood behind the man with the scroll. In pairs, they held three prisoners. Too often, even the weariest prisoners made a sudden struggle for freedom when finally facing the thick rope noose. It was the type of struggle the crowd hoped for. Hangings were as common as weddings or funerals, so without a final bolt for escape or howls of despair, it was a dull event. Indeed, this hanging only drew as many as it did because of the strange knight.

"John the potter's son. Found guilty of loitering with the intent to pick the pockets of honest men. To be hung by the neck until dead."

Most of the crowd shook fists at the accused boy.

He grinned back at them. Ragged hair and a smudge of dirt covered the side of his face. "Intent!" he shouted in a tinny voice at the upraised fists. "Intent is all you could prove. I've always been too fast to be caught!"

The hangman waited for the noise to end and droned, "The unknown girl who does not speak or hear. Theft of three loaves of bread and a bracelet of gold. To be hung by the neck until dead."

The crowd quieted as they stared at her. She in turn stared at her feet. High cheekbones and long dark hair hinted at a beauty to flower— if she were to live past the day.

The tragic air about her forced a mumble from the middle of the crowd. "The baker could have easily kept her for kitchen work instead of forcing the magistrate on her."

The baker flushed with anger. "And how many more mouths

should I support in these times? Especially one belonging to a useless thief who cannot hear instructions?" he asked his anonymous accuser.

Behind all of them—below the small rise of land that held the gallows—the town known as Helmsley lay silent as the spring day began to warm. Although it was important enough to be guarded by a castle, the town was little more than a collection of wood and stone houses along narrow and dirty streets.

The stench of mud and barn animals filled the air. Few of the people gathered on the rise noticed. They fell as completely silent as the town. The strange knight was about to be formally accused.

"Finally"—the hangman in the dirty shirt felt the growing excitement of the crowd, and his voice rose beyond boredom—"the Knight Templar. Found guilty of blasphemy and the theft of a chalice. To be hung by the neck until dead."

The babble of the crowd renewed as each person strained to watch for reaction on the knight's haggard face. *To be so mighty and to fall so far...*

The darkly tanned knight did not acknowledge any curiosity. He had been stripped of all the wealth of his apparel except for his trousers, tunic, and a vest of chain mail. The bulges of his muscled arms and shoulders showed a man who had lived by the sword. He would die by the rope.

He stared forward with a slightly bowed head that hid the features of his face.

The hangman continued. "This on the twenty-eighth day of May in the year of our Lord thirteen hundred and twelve." Finished with his painfully memorized words, the hangman scrolled the useless paper back into a roll and nodded at the soldiers.

To the crowd's disappointment, none of the prisoners resisted. Each had a reason for not struggling.

The potter's son did not believe he would die. At eleven years of age, death was simply not a possibility, even with the knotted rope less than a dozen steps away.

The girl appeared too exhausted.

The knight, resigned to death, perhaps was already back in his land of sun, speaking and laughing in his mind with old comrades.

The crowd grew restless again. Some had neglected a day's work and traveled as far as six miles. Others had brought their entire families. With all attention focused on the three figures slowly climbing the gallows, no one in the crowd noticed a figure approaching from the town behind.

It wasn't until the figure strode amid the usual cursing and jeering that anyone noticed him. Then, the awed silence was immediate.

As it should have been.

No man in the crowd stood higher than five feet and nine inches. This man was a giant, four hands taller than the tallest.

His attire cast a frightened chill among them. The black cloth that swirled around him gleamed with richness and flowed like a heavy river. A hood covered his face; his hands were lost deep in the folds of the robe. He projected nothing less than the shadow of death.

The figure did not break stride until it reached the gallows. Only then did he stiffly turn to face the crowd, confident even with his back vulnerable to the soldiers.

Many in the crowd backed away.

Andrew the hangman, frozen in shock and standing on the raised gallows platform, still appeared shorter than the dark and terrible giant who had walked into their midst.

The huge specter of a man let the silence press down upon the crowd.

Finally, he uttered his first words.

"The knight shall be set free." His voice was unearthly, a deep, rasping evil that sent the crowd back even farther. "He shall be set free immediately."

He extended his arms toward the crowd. One of the children keened high with terror.

The black specter hissed. Blue and orange flames shot from the right sleeve of his robe.

The silence, for several heartbeats, was such that the entire crowd seemed frozen. Then, as if time had resumed again, voices broke out.

"Return the knight!" someone shouted. "Before we all die!"

"Save us now!" pleaded another voice. "Set the knight free!"

The hangman blinked twice, then did something brave for a short, middle-aged man. He pointed at the figure. "Seize the stranger!" he ordered.

Two soldiers stepped reluctantly forward and drew massive, long swords.

The specter turned slowly and waited until the soldiers were nearly able to strike him.

"For your disobedience," the specter rasped clearly, "you shall become blind as trees."

He waved his left arm as if passing a blessing over the soldiers. Both fled the gallows, screaming and pressing their faces in agony.

"Do any others dare?" the specter asked as the soldiers' screams faded.

Andrew, who may have been brave but was not entirely stupid, issued fumbling orders to the remaining soldiers. They, too, drew weapons, but this time only short daggers to frantically saw at the ropes binding the knight.

The specter held his position entirely without motion. His hooded face stared at the crowd.

Then, before the knight was entirely free, a bent and white-haired man draped in faded rags stepped forth. He limped steadily the last few steps until he faced the specter with an unfearing upward gaze.

"I have been expecting you," he whispered so that only the giant specter could hear. "And if you want to live and conquer Magnus, you shall give the crowd *my* instructions as if they came from your own mouth."

Thomas did not reply. Did not move. He was balanced on stilts, and the shock of the old man's words almost cost him his balance.

"Do you understand me?" the old man whispered calmly. "Nod your head slowly, or I will lift that robe of yours and expose the stilts upon which you stand."

Thomas finally gave a nod. How could this old man know?

"Good." The old man's whisper remained the same. "Order the release of the other two prisoners."

Silence.

The old man smiled. "Surely, boy, you have no acid left to blind me. Otherwise you have would done so already. With nothing left to bluff the crowd, you must listen to me." His whisper intensified. *"Order the release of all of them!"*

How had the old man known, too, about the acid that Thomas used?

The specter spoke above the head of the old man. "Release the others or face certain doom," his harsh voice boomed.

The old man chuckled under his breath. "As I thought. You are badly underequipped."

Thomas realized the hangman was unaware of the private drama between himself and the old man and grew brave at his continued safety.

"All three?" the hangman protested. "The sheriff will hang *me*."

"*Do as I say!*" Thomas thundered, projecting the confidence that a specter should.

Not a person moved.

"You are out of weapons, boy," the old man cackled quietly. "How do you expect to force them now?"

His question immediately became prophetic as the hangman dared to protest again. "All three? Impossible."

Murmurs came from the people as they, too, began to lose their edge of fear. A rock, thrown from the back of the crowd, narrowly missed Thomas.

He roared in anger, but without flame or the cast of blindness, it was a hollow roar.

Another rock.

"Old man," Thomas hissed from black shadow, "this is your doing. Help me now."

The old man smiled and looked past the specter's shoulder at the sun. "Raise your arms," he commanded.

One more rock struck the ground at their feet. Murmuring grew.

"*Raise them now,*" the old man repeated with urgency. "*Before it is too late.*"

Thomas raised his arms. He'd extended the arms of the cloak and used sticks hidden by the sleeves to make his arms appear longer than any human arms. The crowd fell silent as if struck.

The old man continued quietly. "Repeat all of my words. If you hesitate, we are both lost. There is less time remaining than for a feather to reach the ground."

The black hood nodded slightly.

"Do not disobey," the old man whispered. "Tell them, 'Do not disobey.'"

"Do not disobey." Thomas added heavy emphasis to his voice.

"I have the power to turn the sun into darkness," the old man instructed.

"Impossible," Thomas whispered back to him.

"Say it! Now!" The old man's eyes willed him into obedience.

Thomas boomed his voice in measured slowness. *"I have the power to turn the sun into darkness."*

A laugh from the crowd.

The old man whispered more words, and Thomas repeated each one slowly.

"Look over my shoulder," he said. "I have raised my arms and even now you will see the darkness eating the edge of the sun!"

Another laugh, this time cut short. Sudden gasps and a few fainting spells in front of him startled Thomas. He fought the impulse to look upward at the sun himself.

The old man gave him more instructions. Thomas forced himself to repeat his words. "Should I wish, the sun will remain dark in this town forever!"

He nearly stumbled at the words given to him, because already the light of day grew dim. "What kind of sorcerer are you?" he demanded of the old man as he paused for breath.

The old man ignored the question. "'All prisoners shall be released immediately,'" he replied in a hypnotic whisper. "Say it now while they are all in terror."

Thomas did as instructed.

In the unnatural darkness, he heard the hangman and the soldiers scurrying into action.

Then he repeated the final words as given to him by the old man. "Send each prisoner from town with food and water. Tonight, at the stroke of midnight, the town mayor shall place a pouch of gold on these very gallows. The messenger I send for the gold will appear like a phantom to receive your offering. Only then will you be free of the threat of my return."

As Thomas finished these words—trying hard to keep the wonder and fear from his own voice—unnatural darkness completely covered him, the gallows, the crowd, and the countryside.

"You have done well, boy. Go now," the old man spoke. "Drop from your stilts and wrap your robe into a bundle and disappear. Tonight, if you have any brains in your head, you will be able to retrieve the gold. If not..."

In the darkness, Thomas could only imagine the old man's hunched shrug.

"These prisoners?" Thomas whispered back. He wanted the knight more than he wanted the gold.

"You desired the knight. As you planned, he will be yours. *If* you prove to him you are his rescuer."

As I planned? Thomas wondered. *How did the old man know?* In his confusion of questions, he blurted, "Why release the others?"

Around them, moans of panic rose as the crowd fled in all directions.

The old man answered, "Take them with you. It will guarantee you a safe journey to Magnus. And you must succeed to bring the winds of light into this age of darkness."

"You cannot possibly know of Magnus."

"You have little time before the sun returns."

"Who are you?"

Thomas wondered later if there had been a laugh in the old man's reply.

His words came through the darkness. "The answer is in Magnus, boy. Now run, or you shall lose all."

FIVE

Thomas slipped from tree to tree in pursuit of the knight, who cut through the forest like a roe deer. In contrast to the stiffness of the stilts Thomas had discarded less than an hour earlier, he followed the freed knight on the leather soles strapped to his feet. His tunic, crudely sewn and badly dyed coarse linen, fit him as tightly as his breeches.

Normally that double reminder of poverty—clothes he must wear long after outgrowing them and the brown of monks' charity cloth—irritated Thomas. On this occasion, while silently dodging branches, he was grateful for the brown that made him blend into the background and happy there was little loose material to snag on twigs and bark.

Thomas glanced up, seeking the sun's position by the light that streamed dappled shadows onto the moss of the forest floor. He made a rough calculation. Distance? Already they were five miles east of Helmsley and the abandoned gallows. Time? Shortly before the *sext* bells that marked midday. A half day of light remained. Yet were there enough hours left to secure the gold at midnight?

Thomas decided he could not risk a delay. He must confront the knight soon. He calculated the knight's forward progress and began a wide circle through the falling slope of the forest to intercept him.

The deep moss soaked up the sounds of his footfalls, and he was careful to avoid dead and dry branches. Around him, bird songs echoed against the hush of the forest.

On the trees, some leaves were still only buds, but others had been encouraged by the warm spring air to unfold. The splashes of green among trees long since tired of winter gave the forest an air of hope.

Thomas did not pause to enjoy the beauty. He concentrated on silent footstep after silent footstep, hoping he remembered the lay of the land correctly.

Fifteen minutes later, Thomas grinned at the sight of a wide stream at the bottom of the valley. While it blocked him, it would also block the knight. A thick fallen tree appeared the only way to cross the water.

Thomas reached the primitive bridge and scrambled to its center. He sat cross-legged and half-hidden among the gnarled branches that bent into the stream, and waited.

When the knight finally appeared, Thomas saw his face clearly. It had been hidden on the gallows by a bowed head but was now revealed beneath the sharp shadows of the midday sun. Hair cropped short— no gray at the edges. Dark eyes. Most compelling was the ragged scar down his right cheek.

Thomas waited for the knight to notice him.

William merely raised an eyebrow when he reached the bank of the stream and saw a boy among the branches of the log.

"This appears to be a popular bridge for a forest so lonely," he said.

It drew a smile from the young man, who added a touch of his own irony. "A shrewd observation, sir." The young man stood and balanced in the middle of the fallen tree. "I shall gladly make room for you to pass, sir. However, I beg of you to first answer a question."

Most men who had fought long and hard to reach the status of knighthood would have been enraged at such insolence. Most knights would have responded with a menacing steel blade. William simply permitted himself the slight curl of a grin.

"What's your name?" William asked. He kept it casual, but this was a more important question than it appeared.

"Thomas. And yours?"

"William."

"You are a knight."

"Formerly a Templar," William answered. A vision came to him of the days when he, like his brothers, could proudly wear the white mantle with a red cross, when they were known everywhere as the most skilled fighting units of the Crusades.

The recent troubles, building for some time, had been twofold. First, those in the order who were not fighters had amassed a fortune for the order, for the Knights Templar had been a popular charity for centuries. But this very success proved a foundation for destruction—the noncombatant members of the order had taken this money and formed banking structures that had begun to threaten the power of kings across Europe.

The kings could not act, however, with such popular support for the Templars, tied closely to the victories of the Crusades. This support had disappeared over the last half century, however, as the Crusaders slowly lost the Holy Land to the infidels. When they had been defeated in their last stronghold on the edge of the Holy Land—a fortified town called Acre, a harbor on the Mediterranean—the king of France, who was deeply in debt to the order, took advantage of the loss. He had French members arrested and tortured into false confessions against the Church, then pressured the pope to officially disband the order.

Too many of William's brothers-in-arms had died not by the

swords of infidels, but by burning piles of wood lit by the very authorities they'd gone on Crusades to honor and protect.

"Your arrest, then," Thomas said, "was unfortunate politics?"

"I refused to renounce my vows to the order," William said. "It is a
common fate for all of my brothers, one I was not afraid to share."

"And—"

William interrupted whatever question Thomas intended next.
He'd shared his own history hoping to learn Thomas's. "Well, Thomas,
from where do you hail?"

This was even more important than knowing Thomas's name. If
the young man was who William suspected, there was much to gain
from the answer. He could send someone back to learn about Thomas's
boyhood and habits. From there, perhaps, the treasure could be found.

"I'll ask the questions, if you don't mind," Thomas said.

William hadn't expected it to be easy, but it had been worth a try.

"You are an unlikely troll." William set down the large leather bag
he had been carrying over his shoulder and contemplated Thomas.
"That *is* a legend in this country, is it not—the troll beneath a bridge
with three questions to anyone who wishes to pass?"

"I am not a legend," Thomas answered, then added boldly, "but
together, we may be."

They stared at each other in a silence pleasantly broken by the bur-
bling of the stream.

William saw a square-shouldered boy, dressed in the clothing of a
monk's assistant, who did not flinch to be examined so frankly. Ragged
brown hair tied back. High forehead to suggest strong intelligence. A
straight, noble nose. And a chin that did not waver with fear at a knight's
imposing gaze.

Then the knight noticed Thomas's hands. Large and ungainly,

they protruded from coarse sleeves too short for their wearer. *Nearly a man, yet still a puppy with much growing to do,* the knight thought with amusement.

What checked the knight's smile was the steady grace promised in the young man's relaxed stance, and the depth of character in the gray eyes flecked with blue that stared back with calm strength. *Does a puppy have this much confidence,* the knight wondered, *this much steel at such a young age?*

Then the knight did grin. This puppy was studying him in return with an equal amount of detached curiosity.

"I presume," the knight said with a mock bow, "I pass your inspection."

Thomas did not flush as the knight expected. He merely nodded gravely.

Strange. Almost royal. As if we are equals, the knight thought. He let curiosity overcome a trace of anger and spoke again. "Pray tell, your question."

Thomas paused, seeming to weigh his words carefully. "Does your code of knighthood," he finally asked, "make provisions for the repayment of a life saved and spared?"

William thought back to his tired resignation at the gallows, then to the powerful joy that followed at being spared by the miracle of the darkened sky. Even though he had expected the old man to appear at exactly the right time, it had still been a relief when the eclipse occurred as they had calculated.

"If there is nothing in this code you speak of," William said slowly as he pictured the heavy ropes of his near death, "I assure you, there certainly should be."

Although he had to pretend otherwise, William now knew this

was the one they had been waiting for. He could anticipate what was coming next and was glad for it. Finally, after all these years, he and the others were on the verge of reclaiming what had been lost for so long.

Thomas nodded. "William, it was I who saved you from the gallows." The young man cast his words across the water. "Consider me with kindness, I ask, in the regretful necessity that forces me to require repayment of that debt from you."

William had always viewed himself as a fighting man, but now he needed to be an actor.

"Insolent whelp!" he roared.

In one savage movement, as if truly enraged, he surged onto the log and lunged at Thomas. His bare hands flashed. Fingers of iron tore into paralyzed flesh.

"I'll grind you into worm's dust!" the knight vowed as he tightened fingers around the neck in his grasp. "To follow me and lay such a pretentious claim…"

William's biceps bulged as he began to lift Thomas by the throat with both of his war-hardened hands. This was a delicate moment. He had to make his rage convincing, yet needed to make it look as though Thomas could defeat him—absurd as the idea was—in hand-to-hand combat.

Unable to speak, Thomas did the only thing he could do. Eyes locked onto eyes, he waited for the knight's sanity to return.

The knight only roared an animal yell and lifted Thomas higher.

Blackness began a slight veil across Thomas's vision.

He brought a knee up in desperation. It bounced off the chain mail stretched across the knight's belly and hidden beneath his shirt.

Still, William squeezed.

The blackness became a sheet.

I...must...explain, Thomas willed to himself. *One...last...chance.* He reached for one of the gnarled branches of the fallen log. *If...this... breaks...I...am...*

He did not waste energy completing the thought. With his final strength, Thomas pulled hard on the branch. It was not much. The knight's rage had already drained too much life from his bursting lungs. But it was enough.

William—already in an awkward position with Thomas held extended in midair—did not anticipate the tug on his balance. Both toppled sideways into the stream.

Thomas nearly made the fatal mistake of gasping for air as the iron hold on his throat vanished. Instead, he bucked against the water and fought for the surface. He reached his feet in the waist-deep water and sucked in a lungful of air.

He looked for the knight, prepared to scramble for land.

Instead of a charging bull, however, he saw only the matted cloth of the knight's half-submerged back.

Thomas reacted almost as swiftly in concern as William had moments earlier in anger.

He thrashed through the water and pulled the knight upward. The reason for the man's state immediately became obvious. An ugly gash of red stretched across the knight's temple. Thomas winced as he noted the smear of blood on a nearby boulder with which the knight's head had collided.

He dragged the man to shore, ripped a strip of cloth from his shirt, and began dabbing at the blood. Within seconds, William groaned. He blinked himself into awareness and looked up at the boy.

"By the denizens of Hades," William said weakly, his sudden rage vanished. "This cannot mean you have now *really* spared my life."

SIX

They began their conversation as their outer clothes dried among the branches.

"You left the pickpocket and the girl at the road." Thomas made it a statement. "And you seek to hide in the forest."

"You followed me," William countered as he hopped and slapped himself with both arms against the cold. "And don't think because I am not strangling you again that I accept your story about the rescue at the gallows."

Thomas moved back to place several more cautious yards between them. "I *was* that specter."

William laughed. "Look at you. A skinny puppy drenched to the bone. Not even as high as my shoulders. And you claim to be the specter who brought darkness upon the land."

Thomas watched the knight shiver. It became apparent the shivering was not from the chill of the spring air when the knight reverently made a sign of the cross.

"Such a miracle I have never heard proclaimed," William said.

Thomas could say little to that. He himself could still only half believe the events of the morning. Silence seemed to swallow them as they shivered in the depths of the forest.

"I was that specter," Thomas persisted. "I stood upon stilts, covered by a black robe and—"

The knight moved to a patch of sunlight. His white legs gleamed. "Don't bother me with such nonsense," he growled. "I heard the specter speak. Your voice is a girl's compared to the one that chilled the crowd."

Thomas hugged himself for warmth. "I spoke through a contraption designed to conceal my voice."

Again the knight waved him into silence. "I see none of these inventions with you."

"I needed to find you quickly," Thomas protested. "I barely had time to hide my bundle."

"How old are you, lad?"

"Eighteen."

"Eighteen," the knight repeated darkly. His voice rose. "Eighteen!" He paused, and Thomas could see his anger grow. "You try my patience, puppy. No man—let alone a half-grown man—has the power to shoot flame from his hands or cast blindness upon the sheriff's best men." William drew himself up. "And no man has the power to bury the sun." He touched his forehead and brought his finger down to examine the blood, then scowled. "If you continue to insist upon these lies, I shall soon forget you pulled me from the stream."

Thomas paused halfway through the breath he had drawn to reply. The forest *was* silent.

He held up a hand and cocked his ear for sound. Any sound.

"Did the hangman make any suggestion that you would be followed?" he asked.

William shook his head, then scowled again. "None. The man was as cowed as any of the villagers. He fairly cried with relief to see me on my way."

"I promise you, William," Thomas said in a low voice, "I was that specter. And I beg you give me the chance to prove it."

"For what reason?"

"That I will not reveal unless you make a vow to help me for saving your life. The help, I humbly add, that you have already promised to the person who saved you from the gallows. Once I prove I am the one who kept you from the rope, you will give me that vow."

William waved a fist in Thomas's direction. "Here is my word. Take the pouch of gold at midnight from the gallows—which, I assure you, will be heavily guarded—and deliver it to me tomorrow in the guise of the specter. Then I shall be in your debt. Failing that—as you surely shall—give me peace."

Thomas grinned. In his careful planning of this day, he had never expected to be shivering and bare skinned, waiting for his clothes to dry, when he heard the words he wanted so badly. Still, his quest was just beginning, and only a fool looked a gift horse in the mouth to check for worn teeth.

His thoughts turned, as they often did, to the childhood songs repeated evening after evening by the one person at the abbey who had shown him compassion and love.

So much to be fulfilled…

A giggle interrupted his thoughts.

William sprang in the direction of a quivering bush. There was a flurry of motion and a short struggle.

William straightened. He held the tiny pickpocket and the mute-and-deaf girl by the backs of their shirts. William walked forward with his double burden, a feat of strength all the more impressive because it appeared that it took him no effort at all. Disgust was written plainly across his face.

The dirt-smudged pickpocket shook uselessly to free himself. "People shouted curses at us along the road. Threw stones and called us devil's children," he said mournfully from his perch in the air. "What had we to do but follow? We are fugitives, dead if caught again."

William sighed long and deep and set them down with little gentleness. "I travel alone."

"We shared the gallows together," the pickpocket said. "And survived it together. Surely God has marked us to be together!"

William spoke with more resolution. "I travel alone."

"Alone?" Thomas said. "And what if the one who has spared your life asks otherwise?"

"That is one thing," William said. "But these two are an unnecessary burden. We owe them nothing. Just send them on their way with a couple of coins so they are able to feed themselves."

Thomas remembered clearly every word the old man had spoken to him at the gallows. He remembered the old man's final instructions. *"Take them with you. It will guarantee you a safe journey to Magnus."*

Whoever the old man was, he had knowledge far beyond what Thomas possessed. Whoever the old man was, he had saved Thomas from destruction. For now, Thomas would follow the old man's guidance.

"They stay with us," Thomas said. "A few coins are not enough to keep them safe."

William shook his head. "You don't owe them safety."

"What's to stop them from following and reporting us to authorities as soon as possible?"

"A sword through their gizzards," the knight growled.

The pickpocket grinned, knowing it was a jest. As for the mute-and-deaf girl, she continued to stare at Thomas. He reached for his damp shirt to cover his naked chest from the girl's dark eyes. Then he wondered why he wanted to stare back. He had seen many of the village girls before, always ignoring their coy glances. Thomas had a future to find, the one given to him during his childhood in songs and fables. No girl had tempted him to look beyond that future. *But this one...*

He shook his head at the distraction and fumbled to pull the shirt over his head. There was much to accomplish by midnight.

SEVEN

"A witch! A witch!"

William, who was enjoying drowsiness in the afternoon sun, his back against a tree, opened his eyes and grimaced.

John, the pickpocket boy, scarcely touched the ground as he dashed between trees and skimmed over fallen logs toward him. "An ugly, horrid, flesh-eating witch!"

This portion of the forest was far from the road and unlikely to be visited by superstitious peasants like the screaming boy. Yet if the boy cried any louder, even village bells would be put to shame and seclusion might soon become a lost luxury.

William glanced at the girl to see if she felt the same disgust at this noise. After all, she too was a fugitive—and who could predict how long until the hangman reconsidered his decision to set them free?

The girl, however, remained sitting on a nearby log, her head down as she stared at her feet. Either she was truly deaf or skilled at acting. Time, he decided, would tell.

William rose. He grunted with the effort, his head still sore from where it had hit a rock in the stream. He'd deliberately fallen so that he could lose the battle to Thomas, but he hadn't expected the rock that protruded above the surface of the water. It had astounded him to discover that in a way, he did owe his life to Thomas. Not from the rescue at the gallows—that had been well planned—but from something as unpredictable as falling in the wrong place.

This told William that too much of their plan, like all battle plans, would be determined by chance. All that was ever possible was to prepare to the fullest.

"A witch! With giant claws and fangs for teeth!"

As the boy plunged into the small clearing, William extended his arm.

The boy slammed into it. "Oooof."

"What is this nonsense you are determined to share with the entire valley?" Despite his determination to be angry, William smiled. The boy had forgotten his panic and, newly diverted, had lifted his feet to hang from the knight's arm as a way to test both their strengths. "And why did you wander far enough to find the witch?"

The boy dropped from William's arm and grinned.

"You slept, and"—he motioned with his head at the girl—"she doesn't speak and barely moves. Was I, too, supposed to act as if dead?"

"You have a sharp tongue," the knight warned. "Perhaps I shall cut it loose and serve it as supper to the witch—if indeed she exists."

The boy's eyes widened as he nodded. "She appeared from behind a bush! And it is not my flesh she seeks, but yours."

"Mine?"

"She clutched my arm and pronounced it too skinny."

"I suppose you then informed her that you knew of fatter game and pointed down the hill to where I slept?"

"She was horrid. How else could I seek freedom? She said your flesh would prove tasty enough."

William returned to the tree, then slid down so that his back leaned squarely against the trunk. Finally, Hawkwood had appeared. But if the girl was not who she appeared to be, it would be best to pretend disinterest.

"A witch indeed." William yawned. "More like an old crone wandering for herbs who even now cackles at your terror. Hmmph. Fangs and claws. What thoughts will you entertain next?"

The pickpocket boy squatted beside the knight. "Thoughts of money well spent." He held out a grimy palm for the knight's inspection. "I removed this from her pocket."

William leaned forward for closer inspection. Sunlight gleamed off a thick gold coin, thick enough that it represented a month's wages for any peasant.

The knight opened his mouth to admonish the boy, but bushes parted beside them, and before either could react, a heavy wooden cane slashed down at John's hand. The boy pulled away, but not quickly enough, and the tip of the cane slapped his open fingers, spilling the coin to the ground.

John danced back, hugging his stung hand under his arm and biting his lip to hold back a cry of pain.

William began to roll to his feet to face the unexpected intruder, but he stopped as the cane stabbed downward between his legs and struck the ground close enough to his crotch to pin his pants.

"Move again," screeched a voice, "and you will be less of a man."

William wrapped one hand around the cane and grabbed the intruder's wrist with his other hand. "Much as I admire your bravery, m'lady, it is wasted here. The coin is yours, and it shall be returned with no fight."

He looked upward but against the sun saw only the darkened outlines of the old woman's face.

"Very well." The screech softened. "As it appears I have no choice, I shall trust you."

The crone lifted the cane, but William did not release his grip until he was standing and able to ensure he would wake as much of a man tomorrow as he had today.

He could now see the woman without the glare of the sun. Black eyes glittered beneath ridged bones plucked free of eyebrows. Her face was greasy; her filthy, smudged cheekbones like lumps of blackened dough. From under her ragged shawl, straggles of oily gray hair emerged. A worn cape covered her entire hunched body, shiny where the cloth swelled on her back over the giant lump that marked her deformity.

William was impressed. Hawkwood had done a wonderful job with this disguise. Such a good job that William wondered briefly if indeed the woman was who she appeared to be.

"Shall I be in your dreams tonight?" the old woman mocked in response to the knight's studying gaze. Then she leered, showing darkened teeth. "Or is there a reason you travel with the young wench?"

William glanced at the mute girl, who watched the entire scene with disinterest.

"The girl, it appears, travels in her own world," William replied. "As to my dreams tonight, if you appear, I shall crack that cane across your skull."

"Such a brave man," she crooned, "to bully a helpless old woman."

William laughed. "So helpless that I still tingle to think of that cane."

"My hand," moaned the boy. "It more than tingles."

William frowned. "Give this woman her coin. You were nearly hung for your thievery earlier. Sore fingers is hardly enough punishment now."

The boy bent to pick up the coin from the dirt, and the old crone cuffed him across the back of the head, then laughed a hideous shriek of delight.

John rubbed the back of his head, held out the coin, and glared.

She pocketed the coin, then pointed a bent finger at the knight. "You are an honest man," she said. "Many others would have killed me for much less gold. I shall favor thee, then, with a gift. But you must follow."

William shook his head.

"It is not far," she said. "Humor an old woman." She moved to the edge of the clearing and pushed her way through a screen of shrubbery.

William shrugged. "Stay with the girl," he told the boy. "I shall return immediately."

When he stepped beyond the clearing, the old crone had already moved deep enough into the forest that he could barely see her in the shadows.

"Come, come," she beckoned. "Quickly follow."

When he reached the shadows, she was not to be seen. He paused as his eyes searched the trees.

There, her shawl. He moved forward.

The shawl hung from a branch. A few steps farther, her cape covered a small shrub. And past that, her shabby skirt.

William hoped it had been Hawkwood in disguise. If not, the old woman was coyly disrobing as she walked. Surely, her promised gift was not herself...

Hearty laughter greeted his puzzlement.

William relaxed. The laughter came from a deep male voice. The voice's owner stepped out from behind a nearby tree.

"William, William," the visitor chided. "To see your face as you contemplated the old woman's favors nearly makes our long absence worthwhile."

William shook his head in wry amusement at the wig of horsehair the man held in his left hand and the wax he was pulling from his face.

"Hawkwood," William said. "My lord and friend!"

"Who might you expect? The prescribed years have passed. You, as promised, made your return. Is it not fitting that I, too, keep my promise?" Hawkwood grinned, then raised his voice to the screech he had used earlier. "Shall I be in your dreams tonight?"

"Scoundrel," William replied. "Few are the hags uglier than you. For a moment, I believed it was an old woman."

"I shall accept that as flattery, for if you can be deceived, then I have retained some skill in the matter!"

They moved toward each other and briefly clasped arms in deep friendship. Then each stepped back to study the other.

Hawkwood, silver-haired, stood slightly shorter than the knight. Although older, his face had seen less sun and wind, and the lines did not run so deep as the knight's. It was a lean face, almost wolflike, but softened by his smile. Stripped of the old crone's clothing, he wore simple pants and a light vest, which although not tight, still gave ample indication of a body used to physical labor. His voice, without the screech, was gentle and low.

"It has been far too long, William. The years have treated you well."

"We are both alive," the knight observed dryly. "Anything more is a gift, is it not?"

Hawkwood nodded. "In our fight against the enemy, yes."

The knight watched in silence as Hawkwood removed the last traces of disguise from his face. Hawkwood winced as he plucked at the wax imbedded in his eyebrows, wax not smudged with dirt like the false cheekbones but a shinier white to resemble the bony ridges that had fooled the knight minutes earlier.

"Would that we had time for me to wash at the stream before we speak," Hawkwood said. "And that we had the time to converse over beer at a tavern like the old friends we are. Such luxury, however..."

"Who is there to hinder us?" William asked. "The forest has no ears. And we have much to discuss."

Hawkwood shook his head. "You must return to your young companions shortly. They cannot suspect I was anything less than a wandering old woman."

"They are children!"

"Look more closely at the girl, William. She is almost a woman. And, I'm afraid, more."

"Yes," William said. "I have my fears that she has been sent by the other side."

"Hear my thoughts later on that subject." Hawkwood began to pace a tight circle. "Were your travels difficult?"

"No, m'lord. Exile still provides the secrecy and refuge we cannot have here. And in the southern half of England, none questioned me." William shrugged. "I knew, of course, as I traveled north that word of my arrival would reach the enemy. But also that it would reach you and that you would thus seek me, as you have. But this far from Magnus, I thought myself yet safe from the enemy."

Hawkwood spat. "Nowhere in England is now safe. The Templars have been destroyed, and all these years they have served as protection."

"With the gallows rope around my neck, the same thought occurred to me. I wondered if perhaps the plan we laid those years ago had failed, and that you might be dead by now."

Hawkwood spat again. "There have been moments, William. Their power grows. It was the play of a child for them to arrange the chalice in your horse's saddlebag and to let it be known that you were a Templar and a heretic."

"And child's play for *you* to arrange the time of the hanging?"

Now Hawkwood laughed. "The years haven't dulled you."

The knight sighed, recalling his fight with Thomas. "Perhaps. Perhaps not. But I find it difficult to believe that the eclipse occurred when it did because of happenstance or because of a divine miracle that presumes any importance for my scarred hide."

"Tut, tut, William. We are not without our allies among the powerful. As you surmised, I did indeed arrange the time of the hanging based on our ancient charts. But is it not God who arranges the stars? A century will pass before the sky darkens again. We could not have asked Him for more in the spring of this year."

William waved away the protest. "You would have found another method had there been no eclipse. That was you as the old man, correct? And Thomas as the specter?"

"It was Thomas. Had he not appeared, I would have stepped forward anyway to use the eclipse as a way to save your life." Hawkwood laughed. "Imagine how Thomas felt when the sun disappeared. I feel pity for how bewildered he must be at the way the event turned for him." Hawkwood resumed his pacing. He stepped in and out of the shadows so that the dappled outlines of leaves appeared and reappeared across his lean face. "Sarah trained him well, did she not?"

The knight nodded. "It took all my willpower to pretend surprise when he found me this afternoon. He has grown much since I last saw him. But I was unable to discover where Sarah raised him. Isn't that irony? She thought we were dead. She was so skillful at hiding herself from the enemy that not even we could find her."

"You know my grief has been a difficult burden," Hawkwood said. His voice became heavy, much heavier than his years. "Yes, against all odds, the boy has grown to manhood. We need what she has hidden, and surely Thomas knows where it is."

"The enemy wants it as desperately as we do." William studied Hawkwood's face. "We finally, however, have renewed hope. I have returned safely, you are here, the boy appeared as Sarah was instructed to teach him, and Magnus awaits its angel."

Hawkwood closed his eyes and winced. "But if Sarah were alive, we would not need to play this game. The books would be ours, and we would know whether to trust Thomas instead of wondering if they have planted him as elaborate bait for us."

"And if Sarah were alive, Thomas could take us both to her, and you would be reunited after all these years." The knight placed a comforting hand on his friend's shoulder. They remained in that silence for several moments before Hawkwood continued.

"I repeat, William, without Sarah we cannot know if the enemy reached Thomas after her death and converted him to their cause."

William raised an index finger to emphasize his next words. "Is it not significant that he sought me out at the gallows? Only she would have instructed him to expect me."

"I have wondered the same. Yet because we don't know where she hid him to raise him, nor when she died, we cannot make assumptions.

What if his teaching was barely begun? What if she died when he was still far too young for the passage of rites where a boy is trusted with knowledge of our cause? And what if they found him instead?"

William closed his eyes in thought. "If not from her, then how could he know of me? Magnus fell long before his birth."

"I pray, of course, that he acts upon Sarah's instructions," Hawkwood agreed. "Yet the enemy plays a masterful game. It is equally if not more conceivable that he has been sent forth to lure us, that he is one of them. Did you hint anything of our plan to him?"

William shook his head. "I played the fool. As demonstration of my ignorance, I told him I needed proof he was the specter."

Their next moments of contemplation were interrupted by a high-pitched cry several hundred yards away. "Wiiiilllliam!"

"The pickpocket," William said. "We *do* have little time."

"He is a bright one," Hawkwood said. "It served my purpose to let him steal the coin, for I then had reason to visit you. But his fingers are so light, I almost did not detect his actions. He is crafty and has spirit. If this were the old days, we could consider teaching him in our ways."

"I have an immediate affection for him too," William said. "Except for now, because he searches for me, and it seems you have much to say. What of Thomas? What of the girl?"

"Wiilliaammm!" came the boy's voice.

William paused. "Will we meet soon?"

"In Magnus. If he is following all that Sarah taught him, Thomas will take you there. I shall go ahead and wait for your arrival."

"The girl? You said the girl—"

"Watch her closely, William. Would not the enemy expect us to arrange to have you rescued from the hanging?"

"Yes."

"Would it suit the enemy's purpose more to guard against the rescue and have you killed, or to let you escape and see where you lead them?"

William took a breath and said in rueful tones, "I am more valuable to them alive and in flight. Thus, they would need some method to track my flight."

"Yes. Is it the pickpocket boy who watches you? Or the girl? Or Thomas? That is why I spent long hours waiting for the proper moment to appear as an old hag. I cannot afford to be seen."

"Wiillliamm!" The boy was near enough that they could hear the crashing of underbrush.

"Guard yourself, and do what Thomas demands," Hawkwood said with urgency. "If he is not one of the enemy, he will desperately need our help."

"I will guard myself carefully," William vowed, "and wait for you to greet me in Magnus, whatever your guise when you next appear."

Hawkwood began to edge into the shadows.

"My friend," William called softly. "If I discover Thomas belongs to the enemy?"

"Play his game until you have learned as much as you can," Hawkwood whispered back. "Then end his life."

ompline. Already.

Three bundles lay beside him. One, a small sack of gold and silver given by the monks. The second, the materials he had taken from the cave. And the third, the bundle of stilts and cloth he had used at the gallows at the beginning of the day.

Thomas could do no more to prepare for his next test. Yet the waiting skimmed too quickly. He merely had to turn his head to see the distant gallows etched black against the light of the moon when it broke through uneven clouds.

If I could pray, Thomas thought, *I would pray for the clouds to grow thicker.*

The gold was not in place yet. He had chosen this place to hide because it was near the road from Helmsley. It would let him see how many men the sheriff sent to guard the gold on its short journey.

Not for the first time in the last few cold hours did Thomas wonder about the mysterious old man who had confronted him at the gallows. In front of the panicked crowd, he had taken great pains to force Thomas to demand more gold than five men could earn in five years. Enough to provision a small army.

Thomas shivered. Not because of the cold.

How had he known Thomas was not a specter but an impostor on stilts? How had the old man known what Thomas wanted? And how had the old man deceived them all with a trick of such proportion that it appeared the sun had run from the sky?

The question that burned hottest—Thomas wanted to pound the earth with his fists in frustration—was one simple word. *Why?*

If this unknown old man had such power, why the actions of the morning? He could have revealed Thomas as an impostor, yet he had toyed with him, then disappeared. Why would—

Thomas sat bolt upright.

For how long had the old man disappeared? Would he suddenly appear to recapture the gold?

Then came another question. Not why—*Who?*

In her dying words, Sarah had given Thomas his quest. But she also left him with a puzzle that haunted him every day.

"My prayer was to watch you grow into a man and become one of us, one of the Immortals."

Who were the Immortals? How did Sarah belong to them? How was he to become one of them and why?

And now it occurred to Thomas.

Did the old man have the answer to those questions?

With that final thought to taunt him, Thomas discovered that time could move slowly. Very slowly indeed.

"I'll not rest until this gold has been safely borne away by the specter."

The voice reached Thomas clearly in the cold night air. By reflex, he put his hand on the bundles. Reassured by their touch, he listened hard.

"Fool!" a harsh voice replied. "The sheriff has promised a third of this gold to the man who brings down the specter. I, for one, have sharpened my long sword."

"I'm no fool," the first voice replied with a definite tremble. "I was there when the sky turned black. The ghostly specter is welcome to his ransom. I only pray we never see him again."

"Shut your jaws!" commanded a third voice. "This is a military operation. Not a gathering of old wives."

After that, only the drumming of heavy feet.

Thomas counted eight men in the flitting moonlight. Eight men!

Was he a village idiot to think he might overcome eight well-trained sheriff's men? And if he did succeed at midnight, what might he face next?

Again, Thomas regretted that he could not pray.

Instead, he silently sang lines from a chant that had so often comforted him in his childhood. A chant Sarah had taught him. She'd shown him how to read and write and how to calculate numbers. She'd taught him herbal medicines. History. Geography. Enough so that when she died just after his tenth birthday, he was able to continue to teach himself. But of all the legacy she'd given him, it was the chant that held the most value to him. His destiny.

Delivered on the wings of an angel,
    he shall free us from oppression.
Delivered on the wings of an angel,
    he shall free us from oppression.

⚜

As the clouds came and went, the mute-and-deaf girl watched from the opposite side of the gallows, intent on the well-armed men setting themselves in a rough circle around it.

She had the power to destroy these men, inflicting death upon them with a weapon none had seen before and would not understand until the last had fallen.

She had a narrow, long tube beside her and a bundle of small darts, a weapon and ammunition easily hidden beneath her clothing. It was a combination that she'd been trained to use with great effectiveness. The tips of the darts were protected by hard wax, for even a tiny scratch would result in immediate convulsions of agony and a slow, shuddering death; she'd seen the poison work on a healthy, full-grown pig. She hoped she wouldn't need to use the weapon, for that risked revealing too much of why she'd been placed on the gallows. Still, she'd been given her orders. Thomas needed to be protected.

The bells for *matins* began to ring. Midnight.

The promised phantom did not keep the sheriff's men in suspense.

It appeared as if from the ground, not more than a stone's throw from the circle of men around the gold.

Ghostly white, the phantom moved serenely toward the gallows. It was merely a full hand taller than the largest of the sheriff's men, not four or five hands taller as the black specter had been. In the dim moonlight, it did not show arms. Nor a face. A motionless cowl covered its head.

"All saints preserve us!" screamed the voice of the first soldier.

"Advance or you'll lose your head!" immediately countered the commander's voice. "Move together or die in the morning!"

All eight men began to step slowly forward with swords drawn.

The deaf-and-mute girl plucked the protective wax tip off one of the darts and slipped it into the blowing tube. She lifted it to her mouth in preparation and waited, holding her breath.

The phantom stopped. It did not speak.

A cloud blotted the moon completely. The men hesitated, then gasped as an eerie glow came from within the pale body of the phantom. A few soldiers stumbled backward on the uneven ground.

"Hold, you cowards," came the tense voice of the commander. The retreating men froze.

"A third of the gold to the one who defeats this apparition!" called someone in the pack.

The phantom held its position.

Finally, just as the cloud began to break away from the moon, one soldier rushed at the phantom. "Join me!" he shouted. "Show no fear!"

The girl drew a breath to fire the dart. She had no doubt she'd be able to hit the man squarely in the back, but she still waited. Surely Thomas had planned something; it was not going to be this easy for the sheriff's men, was it?

But she couldn't take the risk. She made her decision to give the sharp, hard burst of breath that would fire the tiny dart through the darkness, but just before the point of the soldier's outstretched sword reached the outline of the phantom, a roaring explosion of white filled the soldier's face. It etched sharply for one split heartbeat every ripple of the ground for yards in every direction.

The soldier screamed, falling sideways as his sword clattered uselessly to the ground.

Unseen, the mute-and-deaf girl turned her head and let out a breath. She gathered her darts and blowing tube and slipped away. Now was the time to return to the camp the knight had set up, before

Thomas reached it and discovered she was missing. She knew she'd arrive before Thomas did, for she would not have his burden to carry. She had seen what the sheriff's men had not.

No man had time to react. The phantom moaned as it became a giant torch of anger. Flames reached for the soldier on the ground, and he crabbed his way backward, screaming in terror.

The other soldiers huddled in a frightened knot. Each man stared wild-eyed at the flames that outlined the figure of the phantom. They whispered hurried prayers, crossing and recrossing themselves.

"A spirit from the depths of hell," one soldier groaned. "Spreading upon us the fires that burn eternally."

As if in response, the flames grew more intense, still clearly showing the shape of the phantom. And it said nothing.

The men stood transfixed. The last flame died abruptly, and the phantom collapsed upon itself. The men did not approach.

One soldier finally thought to glance at the gallows. The large bag of gold was missing.

NINE

William stirred as a shadow blocked his face from the early morning sun. He had not slept well—the ground was lumpy and cold, and the pickpocket had pressed hard against him to seek warmth during the night.

He blinked open his eyes at a mountain of black that filled the entire sky above him.

"Mother of saints," he said with no emotion. "If you are not the boy Thomas, I am a dead man."

"Your control is admirable," breathed the specter in low, rasping tones. "It makes you a valuable man."

With a slight grunt, William sat upright. His movement woke the pickpocket and the girl. Her hands flew to her mouth, and she bit her knuckles. The pickpocket tried to speak, but no sound came from his mouth.

"Send them down to the stream," the cowled specter said in his horrible voice. "Our conversation will be private."

Neither needed a second invitation to flee, and they were far from sight long before the bushes in their way had stopped quivering.

William stood and measured himself against the specter's height. His head barely reached the black figure's shoulders. A twisted grin crossed his face. "May I?" he asked, motioning at the flowing robe at his waist.

The specter nodded.

William pulled back the robe. He snorted exasperated disbelief. "Stilts indeed."

Thomas leaned forward, and as the stilts fell free, hopped lightly to the ground. He peeled back the ominous cowl. Strapped to his face was a complicated arrangement of wood and reeds that looked much like a squashed duck's bill. He loosened the straps. The piece fell into his hands, leaving deep red marks across his cheeks.

"Much better," Thomas said in his normal voice. He rubbed his cheeks, then grinned.

In that moment, the knight saw the happy face of a little boy he remembered from a long time ago in a country far away—but quickly swore to himself not to that forget the puppy had grown and was armed with sharp teeth.

The knight shook his head and made his voice gruff to hide any admiration that might slip through. "I suppose you can equally explain the fire from your sleeve."

Thomas pulled his sleeves free from his arms to show a long tube running from his wrist up to his armpit. "A pig's bladder," he explained as he raised one arm to show a small balloon of cured leather. "I squeeze"—he brought his elbow down and compressed the bag—"and it forces a fluid through this reed. I simply spark it"—he flicked something quickly with his left hand—"and the spray ignites."

William nodded.

"Unfortunately," Thomas mumbled, "it only works once. Then the bag needs refilling."

"The fluid?"

Thomas shook his head. "I need to keep *some* secrets."

"How did you blind those sheriff's men?"

Thomas lifted his other arm to show a small tubular crucible of clay strapped to his left wrist. The crucible had a long, tiny neck that pointed almost like a finger.

"Another fluid," Thomas explained. "I sweep my hand and it spews forth. It burns any flesh it touches, causing a temporary blindness on contact with the eyes."

"Another secret, I suppose."

Thomas shrugged. "I also have the gold. From the gallows. Is that enough proof that I was the one who saved your life?"

The knight reminded himself that he must play the role of a skeptic. He must make Thomas work to convince him. "Perhaps. Did you use more trickery?"

"*Simple* trickery. Shorter stilts and a white cape around me, supported inside like a tent by a framework of woven branches. The cape was waxed and oiled. I lit a candle inside, stepped back through a flap, and let it burn itself down. It was enough distraction to sneak to the gallows."

In one sense, all of this explanation was unnecessary for the knight, who was aware that mixing common powders and fluids could lead to explosions of fire, noise, and brightness. This sort of knowledge came from a faraway land, knowledge Thomas could only have gained through what Sarah had left him. The knight had watched the midnight events himself, curious as to how Thomas might succeed. In another sense, William needed to play the role of a simple fighting man, unaware of where Thomas had gained the knowledge for his apparent sorcery.

William waited, but Thomas described nothing more of how he'd conquered the sheriff's men, and the knight was impressed that Thomas was trying to keep some of his powers hidden from the knight. It also disturbed the knight; this was exactly what Thomas would do if the enemy had managed to draw him to their side.

Hawkwood's words echoed. *"Play his game until you have learned as much as you can. Then end his life."*

To kill Thomas would break Hawkwood's will to live, yet could there be any other choice if Thomas truly was among the enemy now?

All of this ran through the knight's mind as he maintained the role of a lighthearted skeptic.

"You think you have great intelligence," the knight observed dryly.

Thomas thought of the endless hours his mother, Sarah, had spent coaching him through games of logic, through the painful learning of spoken and written Latin and French, through the intricacies of mathematics.

"I have been taught to make the most of what is available," he replied without pride.

The knight sprang forward with blurring swiftness, reaching behind his back and pulling from between his shoulder blades in one smooth motion a short sword.

Before Thomas could draw a breath, William pinned him to the ground, sword to his throat.

"Your confidence has made you stupid," the knight said coldly. "Not even a fool would disarm himself in the presence of an enemy."

Thomas stared into the knight's eyes.

William pressed the point of the sword into soft flesh. A dot of blood welled up around the razor sharp metal. "And not even a fool would walk five miles into a desolate forest with a king's ransom of gold and offer himself like a lamb to a man already found guilty of stealing a sacred chalice."

Thomas did not struggle. He merely continued to stare into the knight's eyes.

William grimaced as he pressed harder. "And lambs are meant for slaughter."

The dot of blood beneath the blade swelled to a tiny rivulet.

"Cry you for mercy?" William shouted.

Neither gaze wavered as the two stared at each other.

William threw his sword aside. "I was afraid of this."

He took his knees off Thomas's chest and stood. Then he leaned forward, grabbed Thomas by the wrist, and helped him to his feet. William gravely dusted the dirt off his clothes, then from Thomas.

It was his turn to grin at Thomas. "The least you could have done was proven to be a coward. Now I have no choice."

Thomas waited.

"In front of God," William said, "I make this vow. For saving my life, you have my service as required. I ask of you, however, to free me as soon as possible, for I have urgent business."

"Agreed," Thomas said.

In the quiet of the woods, they clasped hands to seal the arrangement. Left hand over left hand, then right hand over right hand.

"Now what service do you want of me that was so important that you risked your life as first a specter, then a midnight phantom?" William asked.

Thomas let out a deep breath. "We shall conquer a kingdom," he said. "It is known as Magnus."

The knight expected this answer, but realized the necessity for reacting the way any other man would react.

"You have lost all sanity! An army of two men against a kingdom?"

"We have the girl and the pickpocket," Thomas said mildly. "That doubles the size of our army."

"And doubles the number of those who will perish. Release me from this vow. I'll not lead you into suicide."

"You still doubt? After witnessing how I saved you from the gallows? After knowing I defeated a band of sheriff's men?"

"This is a kingdom. With an entire army. And worse, it is no ordinary kingdom."

"You have heard of it then."

"The dark legends that all in this land fear? Of course I have. The king of England himself dares not to venture to the castle of Magnus."

"See," Thomas said. "Already our task is easier. Once we gain it, we'll have the gratitude of the king."

"What would possess you to want to do this?"

Thomas set his jaw, and the knight saw a fierce light burn from Thomas's eyes.

"I shall not share that with you," Thomas said. "I have my reasons, and I will die before giving up on this quest. And that is enough for you to know."

The knight could guess the reasons, of course, for if Thomas did not belong to the enemy, then Sarah had taught Thomas his destiny and what he must do to reach it. The knight was glad for the fierce light and the determination that he saw. Unless, he quickly told himself, Thomas was doing what the knight himself was doing. Acting a role. Something the knight needed patience to determine.

"No," the knight said, continuing his own role. "I will not do this."

"I believe," Thomas answered, "your refusal is a matter between you and God, for didn't you just swear a vow in front of Him?"

"Honor," the knight muttered as he dropped his shoulders to give an appearance of resignation, "is often too highly rated."

TEN

Thomas followed the knight up a bank. They had just crossed a stream. John had already scampered to the top.

Behind them, Thomas heard a splash. He looked back. The mute girl had fallen into the water while stepping across the round mossy stones that formed a natural bridge.

He stopped. The knight looked at him and shrugged.

Thomas moved down to the stream to help the girl, for she sat in the water with a frustrated expression on her face.

"Are you hurt?" Thomas asked.

She shook her head in lack of comprehension, completely soaked with water, then reached up with her right hand. Thomas pulled her up. Standing in front of him, she pushed her long wet hair away from her face and behind her head with both hands, then squeezed her hair free of excess water.

In that moment, with her face fully exposed and glistening, Thomas saw how amazingly beautiful she was.

She gave him a hesitant smile and reached for his hand again.

He helped her keep her balance as she finished crossing the stream. Ahead of them, the knight had reached the top of the bank, satisfied that Thomas and the mute girl were clear of the water.

That left the two of them briefly alone.

Her clothes were soaked and clung to her body, and with an involuntary glance Thomas realized she was much more than a girl. He quickly looked away to preserve her modesty.

She pulled on his hand, however, and when he looked her in the face, she kissed the tips of her fingers and touched them to his lips. She mouthed two words. *Thank you.*

As he struggled with new emotions that made him tremble, she walked past Thomas and up the bank.

The four of them entered a small town marked from a distance by the church steeple. A pleasant river ran through the center, a rough wooden bridge connecting the banks.

That was about all that was pleasant about the town, however. Human waste littered the streets where shop owners, who lived above their businesses, routinely emptied their chamber pots from their windows each morning. Half-starved dogs roamed, looking for any scrap of food, artfully dodging kicks from irritated passersby.

Thomas made straight for the marketplace, feeling satisfaction at the weight of the gold coins in a pouch hanging from his neck.

The town square was crowded. Thomas noted with amusement that a noblewoman was bargaining hard for a delicate flea cage, accusing the silversmith of a flaw in the intricate design. A flea cage was a small cube that held a piece of fat. It hung on a long chain from the wearer's neck, hidden beneath clothing. As fleas moved up and down the person's body, they would enter the cage and get stuck to the fat. At the end of the day, the wearer opened the cage and threw out the fat and the fleas.

Thomas found this amusing because she was berating the silversmith for an object that would never be seen in public once she began to wear it. The silversmith didn't bother to argue but simply told her the price was the lowest he could offer, and he was thinking of melting it down to turn into a pendant anyway.

Thomas didn't wait for the end of the discussion and stepped over horse droppings on his way to a farrier.

"Hang on, lad," William said. "I'm a little worried about that look of determination on your face. What do you have in mind?"

Thomas shrugged. "Something I have been planning over many months."

"And something you obviously don't intend to share with me?"

"We're hungry," Thomas said. He pointed at a woman roasting a pig by turning it slowly over glowing coals. "I'm sure the boy and the girl would like some of that."

"Ah, so I've become a servant?"

"I'll be happy to get the food. After I've returned."

"We'll wait then," William said. Nothing in his voice betrayed how he felt about Thomas's curt statements.

Thomas wasn't too concerned about how the knight felt, however. This was not where he needed the knight.

Without hesitation, he continued to his destination, where he found the farrier, a burly, bearded man, beside a black horse roped to a post. The man had raised the horse's hind foot so that the hoof faced the sky. The hoof rested on the man's thigh, and he was pounding nails into a horseshoe.

Thomas waited until the man finished.

"Aye?" the farrier grunted.

"I'd like to buy a pair of horses," Thomas said.

"Aye?" This time, surprise filled the man's face, and he examined Thomas more closely, looking him up and down. "And I'd like to buy a castle, myself. Now that we've shared each other's dreams, what would you really like?"

"A pair of horses," Thomas repeated. He started to reach inside his shirt for his pouch of coins to prove he had enough gold, but someone grabbed his arm from behind.

"Ignore the dolt," William told the farrier. "He's been touched in the head ever since a horse kicked him as a boy." He laughed. "It's probably why he wants so badly to have one or two for himself. To deliver a few kicks in return."

"Let go," Thomas said, trying to pull himself loose. He was astonished at the knight's strength and at the futility of his attempt. "I have plenty of gold!"

"Certainly I'll let go," William said in a laughing voice. "Once I have you back where you belong." He shook his head at the farrier. "He's a nice enough boy but suffers delusions that make it difficult on his mother."

The farrier grinned in return. "Better your problem than mine." He stepped to the other side of the horse and lifted the other hind foot.

William kept what appeared to be a friendly arm on Thomas's shoulder and moved him away, well out of earshot. Then he hissed, "Want us all arrested?"

"I want two horses," Thomas said. He shook himself loose. Rather, it seemed as though William allowed him to shake loose. "It will cut our travel time in half."

"Or perhaps now that you have more gold than you can spend, you want the status that comes with sitting on a horse as all the peasants scatter out of your way?"

Thomas fought a tinge of guilt. He had pictured himself in a noble posture atop a horse's back. After years of enduring harsh treatment by the monks, didn't he deserve the elevation that would come with a horse?

"I don't need you to lecture me," Thomas said.

"How about to give you some perspective that will save your life?"

"I—"

"You don't have a choice in this. I won't tell you what to decide. Ever. But you'd better have as many facts as possible before you make a choice. So my role will be to supply you with facts that you don't have. After that, if you prefer suicide, I'll not stop you."

"Suicide? That's a harsh—"

"Suicide. First, we had agreed that it was a risk to travel through towns. All of us are fugitives, after all."

"I'm no fugitive."

"No? What's a judge going to say after discovering that you assisted the escape of three people condemned to the gallows? You're as stuck with us as we are stuck with you."

Thomas had no reply to this.

"And you were about to flash a year's wages of gold in front of that farrier. Think that wouldn't get some gossip going? Then he'd wonder how someone in garb barely better than suits a peasant managed to secure the gold. He'd have asked plenty of questions after that. If not to you, then to all he meets. And among them would be those who would decide you were a nice fat goose that needed plucking. And in defending ourselves from them, again, we'd draw attention to ourselves. Is attention what you want?"

Thomas shook his head.

"Even if the farrier was discreet and said nothing about a young man carrying enough gold to buy two horses and still have a full pouch of coin left over, you need to take into consideration how much more attention you would draw riding a horse through the countryside. Word would travel far faster than any horse, I promise. Might as well leave a trail of crumbs for anyone searching for us to follow."

"Enough," Thomas said.

"Enough? Hardly. Now imagine the reaction to those at the entrance to Magnus. Men approaching on horseback? Those are the kind of men with enough money and power to be a threat. No, lad, you want to appear weak. The more you are underestimated, the better it will suit you in battle."

"I meant enough said because I was wrong and you were right. You'd made your point. No sense beating me further."

"It felt like a beating, did it?" William said. He grinned. "Good. I meant it as one."

ELEVEN

I 'm glad for a warm summer evening," William said, sitting on the trunk of a fallen tree.

The group had traveled until the approach of dusk, then stopped on a hillside to eat cold duck and cheese and bread. Darkness was nearly upon them.

"You have a reason for saying that," Thomas told him. He sat farther down, not on top of the trunk of the fallen tree but leaning against it. "You always have a reason for everything, don't you? And I'm guessing you are pointing out how pleasant it is because you're about to tell us we'll not build a fire. Best not to attract attention."

"Now that you mention it, there was a reason I insisted on the purchase of blankets," William said.

"Always a reason." Thomas had not departed from the town with the magnificent horses of his dreams but a few knapsacks of sensible provisions. "And the reason for rope?"

"Rope is something a man can always use. That's enough reason."

The mute-and-deaf girl, who lay on her side on the ground, stared at the stars, oblivious as always to their conversation.

"No fire?" John said. He perched beside William on the trunk and gave a theatrical shiver. "What's going to keep away wolves and such?"

"The heart of a brave man," William said, patting him on the shoulder. "And that brave man is Thomas. He'll stand guard half the night. I'm not near as brave, but I'll stand guard the other half."

"No," John said. "I'll take half myself. If three of us each take half the night, it's a burden easy to share."

"But if you add three halves," Thomas began, "the total is—"

William cut Thomas off. "The boy is right. Half the night for you as sentry. Half for me. And half for him."

John puffed out his chest, proud to be included. "And when I see a wolf, I'll yell so loud it will run. And if it doesn't, William has a sword and he'll wake up in time. Right?"

"Of course."

"But how many nights will it be like this?" John asked. "We can't expect every night to be warm. If it rains, we'll want a fire."

"A couple more nights," William said. "Then we'll reach Magnus."

"Magnus!" The mute-and-deaf girl whirled toward them. "Magnus!"

John fell backward off the trunk, scrambled to his knees, and peered over the fallen tree. "She speaks."

"Indeed," William said. "She does."

"She never told us she couldn't speak," Thomas said, happy for the chance to defend the enchanting woman who'd walked beside them their entire first day together in silence.

"Of course not," John said. "If a person says they can't speak, it proves they can. But she pretended she couldn't speak. That's almost like saying so."

"People leave you alone if they think you are mute and deaf and have no wits about you," the girl said. "I'll not tell you the abuses I suffered until I learned to make myself someone that nobody would want for fear of an episode."

"Yet you speak now," William said. "What is your name?"

"Isabelle."

"Isabelle, why choose now to speak?"

"Only to stop the madness," she answered. "Magnus! Surely you've heard the stories about Magnus. We can't go to Magnus. Anywhere but Magnus."

"Tell us the stories." William spoke quietly.

"It contains terrible secrets. Strangers who enter the castle never come out. Their bodies are roasted, fed to the peasants. There is witchcraft practiced openly, so it's told."

"It's just a castle," Thomas said. He wished he'd been able to put more conviction into his voice.

"Just a castle? It once was ruled by King Arthur himself! And you know where he got his power, don't you? From a witch. Merlin."

"How do you know this?" the knight asked.

Isabelle stood. "I've spent years listening. When people assume you are deaf, they talk as if you don't exist."

"There is a grain of truth in her words, Thomas," the knight said. "Magnus is more than an ordinary castle. Witchcraft and cannibalism, those are stories encouraged by those who live there to keep strangers away. But there is a certain darkness to it. Somehow, it remains a small kingdom of its own within the king's realm of Britain. Not that it has ever officially been recognized as that. The lord pays taxes, to be sure, but not once in the last two centuries has any king tried to place authority directly upon it."

"That's because the last king who tried it died a horrible death, eaten as if by invisible goblins," Isabelle said. "Insects crawling out of his head as he begged for help."

William sighed. "No. But the king's eldest son died in mysterious circumstances. And in his sorrow, the king left Magnus alone. And I must repeat, that was two centuries ago."

"Eaten by invisible goblins," John echoed. "That's mysterious."

"What's mysterious is the broad range of human illnesses," William said. "I've traveled the world, enough to know there are dozens of natural ways to die that seem like the act of an invisible hand."

"Nobody visits Magnus!" Isabelle said. "Nobody. It's riddled with witches. I don't care what the knight says against that."

"You'll not be forced to go with us," Thomas said.

"What choice do I have? If I travel alone, I'm as good as dead. Please, please, let's go anywhere but Magnus."

"I must," Thomas said.

"But why?"

"Nothing matters to me more," Thomas said. "And you will get no other answer from me than that."

"If we go to Magnus, then we die," Isabelle said. She stood and turned away from them, her arms crossed, forming a silhouette against the stars. "Screaming, with insects crawling out of our heads as we fight for our last breaths. Don't say I didn't warn you."

John let out a deep breath. "I have to say, it was better before, when she didn't speak."

TWELVE

As they traveled through the forest, John roved ahead with the boundless energy of a puppy, and, like a puppy unsure of its master, he just as frequently ran back to check on the progress of the rest of the group.

Thomas, William, and Isabelle walked in companionable lack of conversation.

The canopies of tall trees on each side of the narrow road made it feel like they were walking through a hallway with an arched ceiling. Although the sun was at its highest point, the denseness of the forest and the thickness of the leaves overhead put them in shadow so dark it felt as if twilight were pressing upon them.

The near silence was eerie too. Birds sang ahead of them and behind them but fell silent around them. Occasionally there would be a crashing sound in the underbrush away from the road, and Thomas could only guess—and hope—it was caused by a deer.

There was no doubt who owned this land. The king of England.

Otherwise, peasants too poor to own the iron for an ax head would have stripped the branches for firewood and pulled out the fallen trees. But the king's land? For peasants, it wasn't worth the risk of imprisonment to be caught off the road. The king's gamekeepers wouldn't even have to find them with firewood in their hands, or more damning, a bow with arrows. Leaving the road was considered intent of stealing from the king, whether dead wood for fireplaces or meat for the fires.

As for the solitude, if there was no purpose in entering the forest, why waste time walking along the road? Peasants often lived and died without leaving a five-mile radius of the huts where they'd been born. They had no need to travel.

Those who moved through the forest on the grassy road in places worn to dirt were those with money. Deep ruts from the thin wheels of coaches were a testament to that.

This wealth made them attractive prey for bandits, men who lived in the forests and saw no reason not to kill the king's deer as needed, men who knew that capture would result in execution and thus had little to lose by attempting brazen robbery. Indeed, all that would stop them from attacking a coach was the retinue of guards a nobleman could hire to travel with him through the king's land.

Thomas was well aware of all this; he'd heard plenty of tales from the monks during their drunken meals, jests about thieves captured and women taken as prey.

Isabelle must have been equally aware. She moved beside Thomas and put an arm through his, clutching him close for protection.

Thomas caught an amused glance from William. He pretended not to see it and matched his stride to Isabelle's.

Physical contact with her was entirely pleasant, and he found himself dreaming about how it might feel if she held him tight, her head against his chest, the softness of her hair against his chin. Or her lips brushing against his.

These daydreams were much more than entirely pleasant.

It irritated Thomas then, when John came dashing back toward them, waving his arms.

"Hurry! Hurry!" he shouted from two paces away. "It's a family! They've been robbed!"

Isabelle gasped and pulled her arm away from Thomas. Another reason for him to be irritated at John.

"Slow down," William said.

"I'm stopped," John replied indignantly. "I can plainly see where you are, and I haven't gone running past you like a madman."

"No," William said in an even voice, "slow down your thoughts. Your voice. Collect yourself. If they've already been robbed, nothing we can do now will help them prevent the robbery."

John frowned at William, then spoke in a dead monotone at an exaggerated slow pace. "Hurry. Hurry. It's a family. They've been robbed." He cocked his head and grinned. "That better?"

"Actually, yes. A panicked man inspires panic, just as a calm man inspires calm."

"Well, thanks for the lesson. But is that going to help the young woman get her clothes back?"

John had been exaggerating, but only a little.

The young woman had long black hair, messy like a bird's nest. She sat beneath a tree, clutching an old blanket around her like a cape. Holes in the blanket showed that one of her shoulders was bare.

"We barely got away," the old man beside her told them. A hood covered much of his head. Gray hair stuck out like straw, and his face, in shadow, was smeared with accumulated dirt and grease. He spoke in a reedy, frail voice. "They had hold of her coat, and she had to slip out of it to run. As it was, they ripped her blouse. And we had to leave

everything behind. Everything. We'll starve, to be sure." The old man
spit. "Bandits."

Thomas felt a sharp jab in his left buttock. He bit off a yelp and
glared at William, who had just used the end of his knife to prod him.

"Eyes to yourself," William growled in a low voice that only
Thomas could hear. "It's not fair, taking advantage of the woman's
indecency."

Thomas looked past the old man and his daughter to the fork in
the road ahead. "Where did you come from?" he asked.

The old man pointed at the road on the left. "There. They were
waiting just beyond a stream. There's a bend, and when we crossed the
water and rounded the bend, they sprang out at us. Twenty of them or
more. It was all we could do to save ourselves."

"Twenty," John said. He held up his hands to count his fingers,
then shook his head when he reached ten. "That's more than this. Even
if William takes ten of them, that leaves…" He thought briefly, but
couldn't come up with the number, and concluded, "That leaves too
many for me and Thomas."

"You'd be fools to tangle with them," the old man said. "Have you
any money you can give us for saving you from grief?"

"Grief?" William said.

"Aye. Now you know which road to avoid. Take the road to the
right and you'll not be trapped. Instead of losing all that you have to
them, perhaps you can give us a pittance as a reward."

Thomas reached into his shirt to pull out his pouch.

He felt William put out a warning hand as he leaned into Thomas.
"It's that bare shoulder that's addled you. Haven't you learned? Keep
your pouch hidden. Turn your back and find the smallest coin you
have, then let's be on our way."

Thomas changed his mind about offering a reward and pulled his hand out empty.

"That's better," William said. "I'm glad I've been able to teach you a thing or two."

"I think instead," Thomas said, "we should take back from the bandits what they stole from these travelers."

Thirteen

Thomas reached the fork in the road before he realized William was not walking beside him but deliberately hanging back. When he glanced over his shoulder in curiosity, he saw that William had a restraining hand on John's shoulder. Isabelle walked behind them, obvious worry across her beautiful face.

"Well," Thomas said to William, half-grinning, half-serious, "I suppose it's better to find out here than at our destination what kind of man you are."

"You're accusing me of cowardice." It was said flatly.

John squinted as he watched and waited for Thomas to react.

"I'm accusing you of walking behind me as we approach a decision. You tell me if that's cowardice."

John swiveled his head toward William.

"Curiosity," the knight said.

"To find out whether I'm a coward?" Thomas asked.

"I have no doubt about your bravery. You've firmly established that. Just wondering which road you'll take after your brave declaration back there. The one with the bandits. Or the one without."

"You heard the old man. They attacked the girl, nearly ripped the clothes off her. Took everything they had."

The knight put a hand on each hip. "Is this a battle that belongs to you?"

"They were robbed."

"It's your duty to correct every injustice in the world?"

"They were robbed! You have a sword and are a fighting man. I have my own sorts of weapons. We can find a way to defeat a few meager bandits. And if we can't, what chance do we have against a castle?"

"Robbery happens every day, and gangs of desperate men are on every road," William said. He gestured around him, indicating the roads. "Why bother seeking Magnus? Spend all your days pursuing bandits."

"I am not on every road. I do not see every crime." Thomas crossed his arms. "But the ones I see, I cannot ignore."

"Do you propose that if, somehow, we defeat these bandits, we herd them like cattle to a local sheriff and have them imprisoned? I thought you agreed that we should avoid towns because three of us are outlaws ourselves, escaped from the gallows. Bringing in bandits will likely result in a return to the gallows, you included for helping us escape."

"We don't need to imprison the bandits. Only take back what they stole from the old man and his daughter."

"All right then; satisfy my curiosity. Which road will you take? The one with the bandits? Or the one without?"

"Haven't I made it clear I am willing to take a battle to them?" Thomas said. "We'll send John ahead to scout their position. Isabelle can serve as bait. I have a few things in my cloak that will help us greatly. You've got a sword and chain mail. Surely you can handle what needs to be done. At best, they'll be armed with knives and cudgels."

Thomas began marching up the road that forked left, the one they had been warned to avoid because of bandits. William, John, and Isabelle followed. They walked in silence almost to the first bend. Thomas could hear the tumbling water of a stream around the bend.

"Good choice," William said. He picked up his pace to walk

alongside Thomas. "I hope you don't mind that I offer you some advice, though."

"What's that?" Thomas was feeling generous toward the knight for agreeing to help.

"Keep your distance from the poor maiden in distress who has begun to follow us." William pointed back down the path, and Thomas turned to see the young woman and the old man rushing up the road toward them.

"Hardly," Thomas said. "She needs to be warned against trying to help. We can do this ourselves."

Thomas walked back to meet them. The old man was leaning on a heavy walking staff.

"Please," the woman said, clutching the blanket to her body. "Don't go that way. It's far too dangerous."

"We are not afraid of bandits," Thomas answered.

"Out here in the forest, there's no protection against the evil of men," she answered. "And it looks like your friends have abandoned you." She pointed up the road.

All Thomas saw were trees, the bend in the road, and the flash of water at the stream. She had not lied. They were gone.

Confused, he turned back. Just in time to see a dark flash, like a hawk striking downward. In that split second, he recognized it as the walking staff being swung at his head by the old man.

With barely more time than to manage a flinch, Thomas desperately twisted away, raising his shoulder to the blow. The impact seemed to break his upper arm.

He rolled sideways and kept his balance, staggering a half step backward. He clutched his arm with his opposite hand, hardly believing how quickly events had happened.

"He's fast," the woman said, grinning.

"Not fast enough," her companion said. The quavering voice of an old man was gone, replaced by the swagger of a much younger man.

"The others are getting away though," she said. She lifted her hands to her mouth and placed her fingers inside her lips. She blew hard and a shrill whistle echoed through the trees. "You complicated things," she said. "We expected you to take the other road."

Two more shrill blasts of that whistling sound.

Then she gave a command to her companion. "What are you waiting for? You know he has more money hidden somewhere."

"Wait," Thomas groaned. "I'll hand it over."

"That's not fun." The walking stick flashed again, but this time Thomas's attacker showed shrewdness. Instead of aiming for Thomas's upper body, he swung low and hard—much more difficult to dodge because it demanded a total shift of his feet, not a mere twist or turn with his feet planted.

The massive blow hit Thomas across his left thigh, and he buckled.

The next blow swiped the side of his skull, and he pitched backward. Blackness threatened to overcome him, but he fought the impulse to collapse into the peace of oblivion.

Instead, completely on his back, he reached into his shirt for a pouch with both hands. It took effort to make his fingers obey. He was able to open the pouch just as both of them knelt beside him.

"Hand it over then, if you insist," the woman said laughing.

Thomas softly croaked out a few words. It brought them closer. His vision had blurred, and it took all his willpower to determine where each of them was. He had his right hand wrapped around the pouch, holding it against his chest.

"Give it up now," the woman crooned, reaching in to pull at his hand.

Knowing she wasn't expecting him to do anything but clutch at the pouch, Thomas flung his hand outward, toward her face. He wasn't trying to strike her, however, and his hand flashed past her nose, continuing toward her companion's face on Thomas's other side.

In a smooth arc, his movement scattered a fine dust from the opening at the top of the pouch.

He was trusting that each of them would take that natural gasp of surprise at the near miss of his swiping hand.

And he was trusting he could roll his face over into the ground before the dust settled.

Nose pressed into the grass, he heard both of them wail in agony—high, piercing screams of panic. He crawled forward, knowing neither of them would be attacking him. Far more dangerous was the dust he'd just scattered. He couldn't breathe any of it himself, or he would be clawing at his own throat.

When he thought he was safe, he rolled over again and pushed himself up to his knees. Both of the bandits were staggering, blinded by the dust, their throats and noses filled with what he knew would be the sensation of fire.

But he wasn't safe yet.

He finally understood why William had framed the question the way he did. The knight had not asked if Thomas wanted to meet the bandits. Instead, the knight had asked if Thomas would take the road with the bandits or the one without. William had been testing Thomas to see if he realized that a trap had been set, to see if he guessed the bandits were waiting down the road that forked to the right.

That could be the only reason the woman had whistled. To draw her other companions to this road and send them in pursuit of the three who had left Thomas behind.

Sure enough. Thomas heard distant crashing of underbrush. Nothing like the sporadic sounds of alarmed deer. No, this was the approach of men taking the shortest line between the forked roads. Men that the woman had summoned with her whistles.

That left Thomas with a simple and intelligent decision.

Conscious of the huge blow he'd taken against his thigh, Thomas picked up the walking stick that had been used to strike him. And as fast as he could, he used it to support himself in a limping run up the road, where William and the others had already wisely fled.

FOURTEEN

Too soon, Thomas discovered that while the woman bandit had been deceptive in many ways, she had not lied about the number of bandits ready to pounce on unwary travelers.

Barely a minute after limping across the stream at the bend in the road, he heard shouts behind him. He risked turning his head.

Without counting—because seeing the large group spurred him to double his efforts at running—he guessed it was close to twenty men. The brief glimpse had shown that as individuals, the bandits were not impressive. This was not surprising, for usually only desperate men turned to highway robbery, and desperate men were men who could not find work because of laziness or physical weakness. The men behind him were like most highway bandits—undernourished, diminished from drinking too much ale, and not accustomed to physical exertion. They were simply a pack of skinny dogs, taking strength from numbers.

Thomas, however, felt his own handicap with every lurching step.

Before the blows that had hurt him so badly across his upper arm, his thigh, and the side of his skull, he could have outrun them as easily as a deer flees from a sickened cur. Now, however, each step was agony, both physically and because of the sensation that he was in a nightmare where pursuers skimmed across smooth ground while his own feet were sucking at mud.

And where were the others? he thought with a degree of anger. He'd saved them from the gallows, helped them flee, promised them a better place to live. Yet at the first sign of danger, they had abandoned him.

Yes, he realized with rage, the woman bandit had been truthful in another matter. Out here in the forest, there was no protection against the evil of men.

That rage gave him extra energy, and he was able to better ignore the pounding pain in his thigh. For a few precious steps, it seemed he was gaining ground on his pursuers.

Then he realized he was deceiving himself. The shouts were growing closer.

He took another quick look. Now they were a mere thirty paces behind. At the turn of the bend, where he'd first seen them, they had been fifty paces away. He'd only be able to stay ahead of them for a short while longer, and there was no time to use any of his devices or powders or to plan something to defeat the bandits.

Was this where his dream would end, where destiny had truly been ready to take him?

Still, he would not give up. And he refused to run himself into exhaustion to make it easier for them to swarm him. If he kept some energy now, some of them would pay the price.

He stopped and turned, holding the walking stick chest-high in both hands, ready to fight.

"No, Thomas!" came a shout from behind him.

John?

Thomas risked a look away from the approaching bandits. John stood in the center of the narrow road, between the walls of trees on each side, where moments before there had been only the grass and the ruts from coach wheels.

"Run!" John shouted, waving Thomas forward. "Now! Hurry!"

Where was that cowardly knight? Thomas wondered. A little boy was not much use in a fight like this.

"You run into the forest," he shouted back. "I'll keep them at bay!"

Thomas heard the bellowing of another voice, a deeper voice. "You stupid whelp, listen to the boy!"

William. Hidden among the trees. An ambush!

Thomas turned again and tried to sprint. This time, he ignored the hobbling pain in his upper thigh, and with renewed determination, bolted away from the bandits.

The brief halt in his escape attempt had reduced his lead to about seven paces. The bandits cursed at him, screaming in bloodlust as they closed upon him. Seconds later, Thomas felt the first grasp of a hand on his shoulder. He shook it free and plunged ahead.

Then came a strange thumping, and the angered curses behind him became startled cries.

A step later, more of the strange thumping. And another step after that, yet again.

"Thomas!" William ordered in a loud yell. "Turn back!"

Thomas spun around to see William at the side of the road, surveying all of the bandits, who were groaning in heaps on the ground.

William waved his sword and swept his eyes from side to side, alert for any bandits to attack. "I'm not more than a pace away from any of you," he said in a clear and calm voice. "The first one to stand loses his head. You'll not feel it, because my sword is sharp enough to fell a tree. But your skull will roll among the others smart enough to remain on the ground."

This threat was enough to freeze the first couple of men already on their knees.

"On your stomachs now," William said. "Every one of you."

One bandit remained on his knees.

John darted out from behind a tree, raced up to the man, and kicked him squarely in the groin. The bandit fell forward in a loud groan, clutching the middle part of his body.

"Anyone else?" the boy challenged. "I've got more where that came from."

Thomas hobbled back toward William.

"Keep to the side," William warned Thomas. "We don't want to be among them where they can suddenly clutch at our legs. John, your services won't be needed anymore, so join Thomas, please."

One of the bandits near William moved ever so slightly. William instantly jabbed the man's buttock, sinking the tip of the sword a few inches into the muscle. He left it there and leaned slightly into the sword.

The man howled.

"Next one is in the ribs," William said. "The rest of you, clasp your hands behind your heads. Noses into the ground. Any man who moves his hands will be impaled on the spot." William kicked the man he'd just jabbed with the sword. "And you. Silence. I'm already irritated as it is. The lot of you have ruined a peaceful stroll through the forest."

Thomas was still trying to comprehend what had happened. Then he saw three lengths of rope stretched across the road, portions of each rope lying beneath the prone bandits. From the first rope to the second was little more than a half pace, and then another half pace to the third rope. He followed the ropes with his eyes, seeing the ends tied at knee height to trees on the opposite of the road.

Thomas grinned, picturing the events that had sent the bandits flying to the ground.

With him as bait to lure the bandits forward, as Thomas passed the ropes on the ground, William would have yanked on the first rope from a hiding point in the trees opposite where the end was tied, causing the rope to hover just above the road at knee height. John would have yanked on the second rope and Isabelle on the third rope.

As Thomas raised his eyes from the ropes, he caught William's broad grin.

"Well, lad," the knight said, "now that we've caught them as you wished, what shall we do with them?"

"You've been quiet long enough to make your point," the knight told Thomas. "You're angry with me. Fair enough. Let's talk."

They'd cleared the forest and had walked for another hour out in the open fields, surrounded by peasants stooped in labor, armed with hoes. Their pace had been reduced by the effort it took Thomas to walk, limping with the aid of the stick that had injured him.

Thomas kept his jaw tightly shut.

"By the way," William said, obviously amused, "I know you're making that limp of yours seem much worse than it is. He hit you with a stick, not a sword."

"And you care?"

"Can't say your tone of voice suits me," the knight responded, "but it's lovely to discover you are still capable of speech."

Thomas reset his jaw.

"The childishness doesn't become you, lad," William said, a little more steel in his voice. "We're all stuck together on this. I made a vow to help you, and I'm not going to let your churlishness cause me to break it. So make the choice to be a man about all of this. If you and I have to agree all the time to be friends, it's not much of a friendship."

"You left me behind." As he blurted it, Thomas realized why he felt so angry. It had been that sense of abandonment. His anger was more at his own fear than at the knight. Leaving the abbey had been like leaving the only family he had. A horrible family, but still a family. This motley group had been together just a short while, but the intensity of surviving the gallows and the fact that they were with him on his journey made it feel like a family of sorts, that he was no longer an orphan. Except they'd fled, leaving him alone again.

This, however, was nothing he was prepared to acknowledge to the knight, so he focused his complaint on something different.

"You're going to argue that by leaving me alone, you were able to set a trap that succeeded," Thomas continued. "But you had no way of knowing that I wouldn't be killed."

"You mean by the poor half-naked woman who drew you with a story that only a fool would believe? And a distracted fool, at that?"

Thomas knew the knight was correct about this. He'd had plenty of time to think about the tale presented by the black-haired bandit woman. Could an old man and a woman have outrun determined bandits? Hardly.

Yes, it had been the sight of that bare shoulder, cleverly displayed, that had been a powerful distraction, keeping Thomas from thinking clearly about the situation. It probably explained why Isabelle had not spoken to him once since leaving the bandits behind, and why instead of showing sympathy for his injuries, she was giving him the same cold treatment Thomas had given the knight.

"You sent me back to the woman and her companion. If I hadn't used my wits, I might well have been killed. It was no thanks to you that I managed to escape."

"Had you been killed by only a pair of bandits, then you weren't worth much in the first place," the knight answered. "I wanted to see if you could get out of a difficult situation without my help." He laughed at the sour look that Thomas gave him. "Besides, lad. They weren't going to kill you. Not with the three of us still at loose to report a murder."

"Perhaps if you had immediately told me you suspected a trap, my head and leg and shoulder wouldn't be so sore. Instead of sending me back to the woman, you could have urged me forward, and I would have helped you with the ropes."

"Did you learn a lesson?"

Thomas grunted in agreement.

"And it was, I suppose," the knight said, "not to trust the stories of people you meet on the road."

"More than that," Thomas said. He spoke with grudging admiration. "I've learned I can trust your motives and your capabilities."

The knight slapped him on the back. "Feels good, doesn't it, to release that anger and make peace?"

"Not good enough to admit it to you," Thomas said.

The knight laughed. "As unlikeable as you are, there are moments I can see it's worthwhile to be your friend." Then he became more serious. "Tell me about the powder."

"That sounds like an order," Thomas said.

"Forgive me. Will you be kind enough to satisfy my curiosity? I've never seen such an effect."

"And you'll likely never see it again. I had to use the last of it on them."

That had been another reason for Thomas's anger. He had no doubt that sometime in the future he'd have a real need for the powder. But now it was gone.

Their rope had been too valuable to use to tie the bandits; besides, to what purpose? After discovering the woman had lied about a robbery, Thomas had lost all need to bring the bandits to justice. Spending a day or two trying to herd the bandits to a local sheriff for the sake of revenge wasn't worth the risk of being caught themselves as refugees from the gallows.

So, bandit by bandit, Thomas had taken a pinch of powder and blown it in their faces as they were helpless on the ground, fearing the sword of William. The results had been as predictable as they were devastating, and the four of them had left the bandits retching and screaming in agony along the road, knowing it would be a good hour before they recovered.

"The last of it?" the knight asked. "Certainly it's an herbal powder that we can gather from a local plant."

Thomas grunted again.

"Ah, so that's not possible," the knight said. "Where did you get it then?"

"Someday, perhaps," Thomas said, "I can reveal the answer to you, but for now, I'll simply ask you to trust me." He paused. "In the same way, William, that I've learned to trust you."

FIFTEEN

The wind, as it always did on the moors, blew strong. Above them, blue sky was patched with high clouds. William led the way along a narrow path cutting through the low clumps of heather. They traveled across the tops of the moors. The valleys below offered too much cover for bandits waiting in ambush.

Behind the knight, Thomas and Tiny John—as they now called the always-grinning pickpocket—followed closely. Isabelle, farther back, meandered her way in pursuit, stopping often to pluck a yellow flower from the gorse or to stare at the sky.

"Take them with you. It will guarantee you a safe journey to Magnus." Thomas remembered the old man's whisper each time he looked back at the girl. Was there something more about her than met the eye?

But, distracting as the mystery in her face could be, Thomas had other matters to occupy his mind.

"This must be the valley," Thomas said for the fifth time in as many minutes. "I am certain the last moor was Wheeldale—for as marked on my map, Wade's Causeway led us there."

"A remarkable map," murmured William. "Few have the ancient Roman roads so clearly shown."

As Thomas knew from Sarah's patient teaching, Wade's Causeway —a road sixteen feet wide that trailed across the desolate moors from Pickering to the North Sea coast—had been laid by Roman legionnaires over twelve hundred years earlier. The speed of movement that the road allowed the Romans had made them a formidable invading force.

A thought struck Thomas. "How is it you know about Wade's Causeway? You profess to come from far from here."

Having local knowledge was not the only thing strange about the knight's observation. Because so few could read, most barely knew past their own family history back two generations. To show awareness of the Roman invasion said something about the knight, did it not?

"Listen carefully," the knight said with a grin that reflected their growing friendship. "Aside from faith and honor, knowledge is the most valuable thing a man can possess, and far more useful than a sword."

Thomas grinned back, but could not help but notice.

The knight had skillfully avoided answering the question.

Silently, William cursed himself. Every second in the presence of this young wolf demanded vigilance. If Thomas was what he appeared, William could not let him suspect he was anything more than a knight, for that would lead to questions. Days earlier, he'd been very calculating about using the point of his sword to threaten Thomas, reasoning that it would reinforce the appearance he was trying to give of a knight reluctantly pressed into service.

If Thomas was of the enemy, he would know William's role but could not know of the suspicions outlined by Hawkwood. It meant that the knight's every action and every word had to reflect nothing more or nothing less than a fighting man under obligation to Thomas.

William slowly swung his head to survey Thomas. "England was only a barbarian outpost to the Romans. From where I come, there are many similar to this."

Thomas looked across the valley again, as if he had accepted the knight's answer. "Where *is* Magnus?" Thomas spat at the endless valley. "I know it is somewhere in these moors of York. Shouldn't we have found a road that leads to it by now?"

William sighed and paused to wipe sweat from his forehead. "You want to do the impossible and conquer Magnus. When facing the impossible, why be in a hurry?"

"It's far from impossible," Thomas said. He shifted the bundle across his shoulders.

The knight did not disguise his snort of disbelief, for as a simple fighting man, he would be skeptical. "We are not much of an army. Only in fantasies do two people find a way to overcome an army within a castle."

"I have the way," Thomas replied.

"Thomas, where were you raised?"

"What does that have to do with this discussion?"

Everything, William thought. He spoke with exaggerated patience. "It must have been in a place where you were shut in a room day and night and learned nothing about reality. You must see the world as it is. Castles are designed to stop armies of a thousand. Soldiers are trained to kill. Magnus, I'm told, has one of the most forbidding castles in all of the land. It will have a small army. There are just two of us."

"Delivered on the wings of an angel, he shall free us from oppression," Thomas said.

William squinted. "Make sense!"

"There is a legend within Magnus," Thomas said. "'Delivered on the wings of an angel, he shall free us from oppression.' I have been told each villager repeats that promise nightly during prayers. It will take no army to win the battle."

William did not interrupt the rustling of the waving heather for some time. He had questions now; questions that only Hawkwood could answer. The nightly promise had not, of course, existed in Magnus when he was a knight of that kingdom. Had Hawkwood, who foresaw so much, decided this was how Magnus would be reconquered?

But Hawkwood could not foresee Sarah's death, and now Thomas might be a double-edged sword. How should he react to Thomas's certainty? As one who knew little.

"You presume much," William finally said, in a gentle voice that did not suggest mockery. "Is there oppression within Magnus? And where do you propose to find an angel?"

Thomas plucked a long stem of grass and nibbled the soft, yellowed end. "I know well of the oppression..." He paused. "It was told to me by someone who escaped from there. She was like a mother and a father. I believe my parents arranged to send her with me when they knew the pox had taken them." He pulled the grass from his mouth and stared into William's eyes. "Her name was Sarah. She was my teacher and my friend at the abbey. The monks endured her presence only because it was stipulated with the money my parents had left for my upkeep. She taught me to read and write—"

Abbey. William was closer to the answer. Perhaps later he would push to find out which one. But to do so now would reveal an unnatural interest, especially when anyone else would have a much different question.

William shook his head in postured amazement and asked in response what would be expected. "Latin?"

"And French," Thomas confirmed. "Sarah told me it was the language of the nobles and that I would need it when..."

"When?"

"When I took over as lord of Magnus."

"What right have you to take this manor and castle by force?"

"The same right," Thomas said, suddenly cold with anger, "that the present lord had when he took it from Sarah's parents."

Sixteen

During the next half hour of walking, Thomas said little. The knight remained beside him, seeing no need to force conversation. Isabelle still trailed them, showing she had no desire to get nearer to Magnus. Only Tiny John showed enthusiasm, as if they were on an adventure.

"It must be close!" John said. "Let me get on your shoulders, William! I'll get a good see from there."

William groaned. "I feel like enough of a packhorse without my steed. To be arrested falsely for a chalice I didn't steal is one thing. But to lose my horse and armor to those scoundrels…" He caught the anxiety that Thomas betrayed by chewing his lower lip. The knight sighed, a habit he had formed since meeting Thomas. "Tiny John, get on my shoulders, then." William shook his forefinger hard at the imp. "*Without* taking a farthing from my pockets. I've had enough trouble with you already."

Tiny John only widened his eternal grin and waved a locket and chain at William, who felt his own neck to reassure himself that it was not his.

"It's Isabelle's," Thomas said. "Tiny John took it from her this morning. I didn't have the heart to make him give it back yet. And she hasn't noticed anything all day…"

William kept his face straight. The only reason Thomas would have overseen the theft was because he spent so much time glancing at the girl.

Tiny John tossed the locket to the knight. William glanced at it idly, then felt as if a hand had wrapped around his throat. *The symbol!*

He knew now who had been sent to spy. The question remained, was she a partner with Thomas? Or was he ignorant of the danger?

"A peculiar cross emblem," William mumbled as those thoughts raced through his mind. He, too, had learned acting skills. "Nothing I've seen before."

Tiny John did not give him time to finish wondering. He darted to the knight's back, then scrambled upward to his broad shoulders and shaded his eyes with his left hand to peer northeast into the widening valley.

Tiny John whistled. "I've caught the spires! Far, far off! But we can make it by eventide."

"Only if I carry you, urchin," William grunted. "And already you're far too heavy for a knight as old as I."

Tiny John dropped lightly to the ground and kept pointing. "That way, Thomas! I'm sure I saw the castle that way!"

Thomas said nothing. It was obvious by his eyes that he was mesmerized in thought.

William glanced at the girl, still several hundred yards back. He handed Tiny John the thin chain and locket. "Return this to her. Yet do not let her know that it was on my instructions or that I have seen it. Thus…" The knight searched for an insignificant reason that would not give Tiny John cause to think any more of the incident. "It will appear to her that you have honor, you scoundrel. Then, Tiny John, keep pace! We will do our best to reach Magnus before nightfall."

Tiny John had been right. With the easy downhill walk, it took them less than four hours to reach the final crest that overlooked the castle of Magnus. The bells inside the walls surrounding the castle rang to celebrate the church service of *none*—three in the afternoon.

They paused at the crest to comprehend Magnus as it stretched out before them.

"All saints preserve us," breathed William in awe. "Our mission is surely one of suicide."

Even Thomas faltered. "The army—I have been told—is not large."

William laughed a strained whisper. "Why maintain an army when you have a fortress like *that*?" He spread out his arms. "From afar, I wondered about the wisdom of a castle that did not take advantage of height to survey the valley. Now I understand. A force as large as one thousand might be useless in an attack against Magnus."

The valley around Magnus differed little from those they had been seeing for the previous three days of travel. The hills were steeper, perhaps, but the grass and woods in the valley bottom were equally rich and dotted with sheep and cattle.

Magnus stood on an island in the center of a small lake. High, thick stone walls ringed the entire island and protected the village inside. The keep of the castle—home of the reigning lord of Magnus—rose high above the walls, but safely inside, far away from the reach of even the strongest catapults.

At the north end, a narrow finger of land reached the island. Just before the castle walls, however, it was broken by a drawbridge no wider than a horse's cart. Even if an army managed to reach the lowered

drawbridge, soldiers would only be able to cross three or four abreast—
easy targets for the archers on the walls above.

Water, of course, was available in almost infinite amounts. Lack of
food might be the castle's only weak point, because siege was obviously
the only way to attack Magnus. With the foresight to store dry foods,
the reigning lord of Magnus would never suffer defeat.

For several minutes, Thomas could only stare at his impossible
task. He forced himself to remember and believe the plan given to him
by Sarah.

He hoped the doubt in his heart would not reach his words. Wind
carried each one clearly to the knight. "If it is so obvious to a military
man such as you that a host of armies cannot take Magnus by force
from the outside," Thomas said, "then the way it *must* be conquered is
from the inside."

"That's like saying the only way to fly is to remain in the air," William said. "Of course it can only be conquered from the inside. That's
the only way to conquer any castle. Our first question is how to get an
army. Then we can face the usual question of how to get that army
inside."

"There is something wonderful about a castle this impossible to
overcome." Thomas smiled. "Once we have it, it will be that much
easier to keep."

He marched forward.

SEVENTEEN

William watched as Thomas returned to a stand of trees near the north end of the lake. Thomas was still limping as a result of the bandit attack. Now he moved without the burden of the bundle he had carried during their travels; obviously he'd decided to hide it before the final approach to Magnus.

"I think," William said as greeting to Thomas, "it would serve us well to hide any signs of my trade."

"Can it be that serious?" Thomas asked.

"More than you might imagine. Whatever your nurse taught you in that abbey could not have shown you how drastically the earls and lords of a land guard against any threats to their power."

"But against a single man? I would have thought rebellion in the form of a peasant army or even a gathering of knights..."

William shook his head and lowered his voice. "Now is not the time to explain. Let it suffice to say that serfs and peasants have so little training and so little weaponry that they are considered harmless. So harmless that one man with training or weapons can rise far above an entire village in potential for danger." William paused. "Aside from the expense of a war horse—five years' wages—why do you think it is so difficult to reach the status of a knight? And why there are so few in the land? Those in power limit the number of knights—for their own safety, should the knights rebel."

Thomas considered this and drew a breath to speak.

William waved him quiet.

On foot without lance or horse, without full armor or following squire to tend his gear, William did not at first glance appear to be a knight. After the rescue at the gallows, the sheriff's men had fled in terror, leaving behind only one of his swords and a leather bag—possessions, no doubt they had been hoping to keep for themselves. Sun's disappearance or not, no sheriff would dare risk an earl's displeasure by sending a knight with unknown allegiance forth into the land in full fighting gear.

William smiled a tight smile of irony. As much as he regretted the absence of the rest of his equipment, this was one moment he did not mind being without. A knight who did not declare himself as such when approaching the castle of a strange earl or lord could expect immediate death if discovered.

However, William did not feel safe from notice. The guards at the gate would be trained to search for the faintest military indications of any approaching stranger. The chain mail covering his belly, of course, was an immediate giveaway. William drew his shirt tighter and checked for any gaps that might betray the finely worked iron mesh. To be totally risk free, he should abandon the chain mail, but then he would be as vulnerable to the thrust of a sword as a piglet before slaughter.

His short sword—of the type favored for close combat since the time of the mighty Roman legions—hung in a scabbard tightly bound to his back between his shoulder blades. Once again, it would have been much safer to leave the sword behind, but it would also be next to impossible to find a weapon inside the castle walls. William would have to risk being searched.

And he could lessen the chances of search.

William dropped his cloak onto the ground and pressed it into the soil with his boot. He wrapped himself again without shaking it clean. He smudged dirt into his face and ran debris into his hair.

"Show no surprise when I become a beggar," William warned. He turned to Tiny John with a savage glare. "Stay behind and hold the girl's hand. One word, urchin, and you'll become crow bait."

Tiny John gulped and nodded.

The four of them made a strange procession as they moved from the cover of the trees to the final approach into Magnus.

"No castle is stronger than its weakest part," William grumbled as they reached the finger of land that stretched from shore to the castle island. "And generally that is the gatehouse entrance. This does not bode well for your mission."

Tiny John remained several steps back with the girl, head craned upward to take in the spires. His constant grin was dampened by those cold shadows. As for Isabelle, she said nothing. She'd protested frequently during the journey, but by now it was obvious her protests were useless. Still, anger and fear were obvious by the expression on her face. She'd finally insisted that if they were going to drag her into the castle, they all would pretend again that she was deaf and mute. She retreated back into her silence.

"Expert military advice?" Thomas said.

"Not advice. Sober caution," replied William. "Unless a man can swim"—he snorted—"which is unnatural for any but a fish, as the lake is impossibly wide."

"Nobody *swims* across," Thomas argued. "That's why there's a drawbridge."

"Not swimming *toward* the castle. *Away.* Defenders often force attackers into the water. Those who can't swim drown. Those who can swim, cannot fight."

William shuddered. "Especially weighed down with armor." William pointed farther away from the castle. "Worse, this road is the only approach to the castle, and I've never seen a barbican that stretches an entire arrow's flight from the drawbridge to the gatehouse. And nearly straight up!"

Lined with small stone towers on each side—small only in comparison to the twin towers of the gatehouse itself—thick walls guarded a steep approach to the castle entry.

"If this gives a hint of the defenses, I can only guess at the treacherousness of the gatehouse itself," William said. He opened his mouth to say something, then paused as a new thought struck. "Not even *vespers,* the sixth hour past noon. Yet this road is as quiet as if it were already dusk. No passersby. No farmers returning from the fields. No craftsmen to or fro. What magic keeps this castle road so quiet?"

"What does it matter?" Thomas shrugged. "All we need to do is get within the walls as any passing strangers seeking a night's rest. From there, we shall find the weakness of Magnus and complete my plan. As I have said, once we have this, it only makes it easier for us to keep—"

"Don't be a blind fool," snapped William. "I am bound to you by a vow, but I will not follow you to certain death. Lords of manors like this have power and wealth beyond your greatest imagination. Inside those walls will be soldiers to jump at his every whim. It is a rule of nature that when men have power, they use it with joy, and also use it mercilessly to keep it."

"William," Thomas said, unperturbed by the knight's sudden anger, "not once have I given you any indication that I expected you to fight. I simply need your military knowledge."

Thomas thought of his book, still hidden safely at the abbey. "With you as advisor, I have ways of using my own powers…"

"Then we shall proceed to the gatehouse," William said. "But slowly. I do not like this situation at all."

Eighteen

As they began the journey across the narrow finger of land to the drawbridge, Thomas watched as William began to drag one foot and work enough spit into his mouth so that it drooled from his chin.

A huge lattice wall of wood meshed with iron bars hung head high above the first opening past the drawbridge. Each iron bar ended in a gleaming spike.

"Not good," William whispered. "Someone cares enough to maintain those spikes in deadly order. An indication of how serious they are about security." He motioned his head briefly at the shadows of two men standing at the next gate at the end of the stone corridor that ran between the portals. "All those soldiers beyond need to do is release a lever, and those spikes crash down upon us like a hammer of the gods."

Thomas held his breath. The gate remained in place as they passed beneath.

William maintained his whispered commentary as he trudged and leaned heavily on Thomas. "Look above and beside. Those slots in the stone are called 'murder-holes.' Designed for spear thrusts, crossbow arrows, or boiling liquids from hidden passages on the other side."

Thomas tried not to wince.

With his dragging foot, the knight tapped a plank as wide as two men imbedded in the stone floor. "It drops to a chute, probably straight to the dungeon."

The knight took two more slow and weary steps, then paused, as if for rest, just before earshot of the two guards. He spoke clearly and softly from the side of his mouth in the dark corridor as he wiped his face in pretend fatigue.

"Thomas, the outside defenses of this castle are as fiendish and clever as I've seen. It does not bode well for any man's chances on the inside. There is only you and me. Something impossible like this…" William hesitated and lightly touched the scar that ran jaggedly down his cheek. "You may still turn back with honor. And live."

Thomas felt very young as he stared at the broad shoulders of the first soldier at the gate.

Night after night in the darkness of the abbey, lying on a straw bed during his waking dreams of glory, it had seemed so easy. Now, in the harshness of the sunlight and the dust and the noise of the village beyond the stone-faced soldiers, it seemed impossible. Not even the solid presence of William helped.

The guards blocked a narrow entrance cut into the large gate. Dressed in brown with a wide slash of red cloth draped across their massive chests, each stood as straight and as tall as the thick spears they balanced beside them.

"Greetings to you," William said in a hopeful, almost begging tone.

The guards barely grunted to acknowledge the arrival of the newcomers. Thomas forced himself to look away from the cold eyes of the soldiers.

Suddenly, the guard on the right whirled and tossed his spear sideways at William.

"Unnnggghh," the knight said weakly. He brought his left hand up in an instinctive and feeble motion to block the spear that clattered across his chest. The effort knocked him back, and William sagged to his knees.

"I beg of you," he moaned as spit dribbled from the side of his mouth. "Show mercy."

The soldier stood over him and studied the knight's dirty cloak as William cowered.

Thomas remembered William's earlier advice about the advantage of an enemy who underestimates. And he remembered a passage from one of his precious hidden books, a thought written by the greatest general of a faraway land who had lived and fought more than fourteen centuries earlier.

One who wishes to appear to be weak in order to make his enemy arrogant must be extremely strong. Only then can he feign weakness.

Thomas grinned inside. He felt fractionally more confident than he had upon approaching the gate.

Finally, the soldier sneered down at William. "Mercy indeed. It's obvious you need it. Get up, you craven excuse for a man."

William wobbled back onto his feet. The spit on his chin showed flecks of dirt.

"Lodging for the evening," the knight pleaded. "We are not thieves. I am but a worker seeking employment to support my family." He gestured at Thomas and the other two, as if they were his children. Then fumbled through his leather waist pouch and pulled free two coins. "See, we have money for lodging. We ask no charity of the lord of the manor."

The second soldier laughed with cruelty. "Make sure it is cleaning and slopping you seek. Not begging, as it appears."

The first soldier kicked William. "Up. Get inside before we change our minds."

William howled and held his thigh where the soldier's foot had made a sickening thud. He hopped and dragged his way inside the gate without looking back to see if Thomas and the two children followed. Thomas pushed Tiny John and Isabelle ahead of him.

Not until they had turned past the first building inside did William stop. He waited and watched Thomas with a proud chin and guarded eyes.

Thomas did not let him speak.

"Artfully done," Thomas said. "By using your left hand instead of the right when he threw that spear, you made it impossible for them to guess you are an expert swordsman."

William motioned for them to continue walking. "I like this less and less," he said in a low voice. "When I showed those coins, I expected greed would force the soldiers to demand a bribe for our entry. They did not."

Thomas raised a questioning eyebrow.

"Corruption shows weakness, Thomas. We are now inside, and everything points to unconquerable strength."

NINETEEN

Thomas usually slept lightly. Years of constant awareness in the abbey had taught him to do so. Here, in strange lodgings, with a fortune of gold hidden in his leather pouch, he expected even the slightest shifting of movement would have pulled him from slumber.

He woke as first light nudged past the wooden crossbeams of the crude windows high on the dirty stone wall of the stable where they had found shelter and was surprised to discover Isabelle gone. Somehow she slipped away without his notice.

Thomas did not stop to wonder why his first waking thoughts—and his first waking glance—had turned to her.

At least a dozen times each day, Thomas realized that only the girl's poor rags and intermittent spasms had hindered grown men from staring at her with open admiration. Her role as a deaf-and-mute girl seemed more and more like a good strategy to defend herself.

Thomas rose to his feet.

"She's gone," he blurted, noticing William awake beside him.

"She is indeed," William replied. "It happens that way."

"That's it? You care so little about her that you make a vague philosophical statement like that?"

"Shall we start searching for her?" William asked as he stood and stretched away his sleep. "She's gone by her own choice. If we find her, are you going to drag her back and force her to be with us like a prisoner?"

"No," Thomas lied. "I don't care that much."

Thomas adjusted his clothing as a way to struggle through an ache he couldn't explain.

Tiny John merely sat up, hunched against his knees in his corner position, and grinned at the world.

I'm in Magnus, Thomas thought. *With a task that threatens my life, will test everything I have been taught, and demands that I use every power available to me. Yet my mind turns to sadness. How could that have happened?*

Isabelle pushed open the door by walking backward through it. When she turned, the bowls of steaming porridge in her hands gave obvious reason for her method of entry.

She looked shyly at Thomas and smiled as she offered him a bowl, saying nothing.

I shall conquer the world, Thomas finished in his mind.

"The walls of Magnus contain no mean village. There must be nearly five hundred inside," William said. "I'm surprised it has no fame outside this county."

And I'm more surprised, William thought anxiously, *that there was so little traffic on the road during our approach. The enemy has so thoroughly taken Magnus that the entire countryside appears to be in its power.*

He did not voice his worry. It might not have mattered anyway, as it appeared Thomas was not listening. He was too busy staring in all directions to reply. If the boy had been raised in an abbey in the countryside as he said, William could imagine his awe. No village could compare to this.

Already the clamor in Magnus was at a near frenzy.

"Fresh duck!" a toothless shopkeeper shouted as he dangled a bird by the feet in one hand and waved at Thomas with the other. "Still dripping blood! And you'll get the feathers at no charge!"

Thomas smiled politely and pushed ahead of the knight. Tiny John and Isabelle followed, staying close to William. Shops crowded the street so badly that in occasional places, crooked buildings actually touched roofs where they leaned into one another. Space among the bustling crowd was equally difficult to find.

William scanned the buildings for identification. There was the apothecary, marked by a colorfully painted sign displaying three gilded pills. He made a note to remember it. The potions, herbs, and medicines inside might be needed on short notice. A bush sketched in dark shades—the vintner, or wine shop. Two doors farther along, a horse's head—the harness maker. Then a unicorn—the goldsmith. A white arm with stripes—the surgeon-barber.

There was a potter, a skinner. Shoemaker. Beer seller. Baker. A butch—butcher.

William grimaced and pulled his foot away from the puddle of sheep's innards that had been thrown into the middle of the street. Butchers did their slaughtering on the spot for customers and left behind the waste for the swarms of flies already forming black patches on nearby filth.

"Where is it we go?" Thomas called.

"A stroll," William said. "I have a few questions that simple observation should answer."

At the end of the first street, they turned left, then left again to follow another crooked street. It took them away from the market crowd and past narrow and tall houses squeezed tightly together.

"Well, Thomas," the knight said, "is it all you expected it to be?"

"As long as we are able to continue to walk freely," Thomas said, "how much danger can there be?"

Isabelle caught up to Thomas. He remembered what Sarah had taught him about manners and quickly moved so that he walked on the outside, ensuring Isabelle stayed nearer the houses. Thus, if a housewife emptied a jug of water or a chamber pot onto the street from the upper stories, Thomas would suffer, not Isabelle. She seemed content to stay beside him, glancing over to smile whenever Thomas stared at her for too long.

In contrast, Tiny John burned with energy and scampered in circles around them. First back to William, then ahead to Thomas and the girl.

"Check his pockets," William said without breaking stride. "If that little rogue so much as picks a hair from a villager, all of us are threatened."

Tiny John stuck out his tongue at the knight but quickly pulled his pockets open to show he'd managed to remain honest.

More walking.

Thomas sniffed the air with distaste. They were approaching the far edge of the town—the traditional location of the tannery. Thomas knew the procedure too well. How many times had one of the monks at the abbey ordered him to scrape hair and skin from the hide of a freshly killed sheep? As many times as they had then ordered him to rub it endlessly with cold chicken dung. That ingredient, plus the fermented bran and water used to soak the hides, made it an awful job.

They walked by the tannery quickly. Thomas felt sympathy as he watched one of the apprentices scraping flesh, mouth open to keep his nostrils as useless as possible.

The street turned sharply, and within a few hundred more paces, they were back within earshot of the market. Just before reaching the market area, William held up his hand.

"Thomas," he said with low urgency. "Look around. What strikes you?"

Thomas had a ready reply. "The crippled beggars. The men with mutilated faces. Far more than one would expect."

The knight's eyes opened wide. "My mind was on military matters. I had not noticed. Surely the lord of Magnus hasn't..."

Thomas shrugged. "I have been told many stories of the evil here." In his mind, he heard Sarah singing gently: *Delivered on the wings of an angel, he shall free us from oppression.*

William said, "Scan the shop signs. Tell me what's missing."

"Missing?"

The knight only frowned in thought. Thomas began to study the busy scene ahead.

Finally he answered. "I see no blacksmith."

"You speak truth. Why is that significant?"

Thomas had a flash of comprehension. "Horseshoes and hoes are not the only items a blacksmith makes. Blacksmiths also forge swords. Without a blacksmith, there are no weapons. No armor. Whoever controls Magnus takes few chances."

"Well spoken."

Before William could comment further, a small man broke toward them from the fringes of the crowd. His shoulders were so insignificant they were nearly invisible under his brown full-length cloak. A tight black hat emphasized the smallness of his head. His wrinkled cheeks bunched like large walnuts as he smiled.

"Strangers!" he cackled. "So brave to visit Magnus, you are! No doubt you'll need a guide. No doubt at all!" He rubbed his hands briskly. "And I'm your man. That's the spoken truth. No doubt. The spoken truth."

Thomas made a move to step around him, but William shook his head at Thomas, then addressed the small man.

"What might be your name, kind man?"

"Ho, ho. Flattery. Always wise. Indeed, you are fortunate. I am a kind man." The small man paused for breath, winded by his rapid-fire words. "And I am called Geoffrey."

"Hmm. Geoffrey. You are a merchant?"

"Indeed I am. But strangers are wise to engage a guide in Magnus. And I make a fine guide. A fine guide indeed."

"Any man can see that." William smiled. "What is it you sell when you are not a guide?"

"Candles. Big ones. Little ones. Thick ones. Skinny ones. The finest in the land. Why, the smoke from these candles will wipe from a window with hardly any—"

"Sold." William jammed his single word into the pause that Geoffrey was forced to take for breath.

"Sold?" Geoffrey's confidence wavered at this unexpected surrender. "I've not shown a one. How can you say—"

"Sold," William repeated firmly. He pulled a coin from his pouch. "Maybe even as many as we can carry." He peered past Geoffrey's shoulders. "Where might your shop be?"

Geoffrey opened and closed his mouth like a fish gasping for air. He did not take his eyes from the coin in William's palm. "My...my shop is away from the market. I only bring enough candles for the morning's sales. I..."

"Lead on, good man," William said cheerfully. "It's a pitiable guide who cannot find his own shop."

Geoffrey turned and excitedly led the way through the market crowd. Every five steps or so, he rudely pushed people aside despite his runtlike size. The resulting arguments proved to be a humorous distraction. Thomas took advantage of the noise to address the knight.

"He's a blathering fool," Thomas whispered to William. "What do you want from him?"

"Certainly not candles," William whispered from the side of his mouth. "I want a safe location to ask questions."

Thomas could not fault the knight for his strategy. Yet must the information come from an empty-headed babbler?

TWENTY

As the others followed the candle merchant through the crowd, Isabelle drifted away to stand in the shadows of a doorway. A hunched beggar approached her. His face was obscured by dirt, and he held out a filthy hand, as if begging.

His words, however, did not match his actions. "Sacrifices must be made beneath a full moon."

"And a full moon shines upon us with favor," she answered.

The beggar grunted satisfaction that she had not shown any surprise.

"Does Thomas suspect you are anything but what you appear to be?" he asked.

"He suspects nothing." Isabelle fumbled with a pocket, searching for a coin. "I even pretended great fear upon learning this was his destination."

"What have you learned?" the beggar asked.

"He dreams of conquering Magnus," she answered.

"That much is obvious," the beggar said. "I want to know how he intends to attempt this."

"He has said nothing to the knight within my hearing."

"And to you? Surely you've found opportunity to tempt him. He's as hot-blooded as any man. If you can't turn his heart, then his heart doesn't exist. Has he confided anything to you?"

"He keeps his distance," she answered. "When I try to spend time alone with him, he moves away. As if he is afraid of allowing himself to be close to me and that I will be too much of a distraction as he pursues the conquest of Magnus."

"So you do have power over him?"

"Given time, yes, his heart will be mine. But he says nothing. He is secretive."

"We don't have time. He has what we want, and it gives him too much power. We cannot lose Magnus. Visit him in the prison."

"Prison!"

"He will be there soon. Speak to him and offer him comfort."

Isabelle drew a breath. "Do I reveal who I am, then?"

The beggar said, "Hint that you have a secret to protect. A great secret. That you have protected yourself by trying to remain invisible. Hint that you have enemies and that you need his protection. A man such as he will move heaven and earth for a beautiful woman who appeals for help. If you can, let him know that you desire him."

"To what end?"

"You have been raised as one of us, but you are also a woman. Could you see yourself with him? No, let me answer that. I can see in your eyes how you feel about him. Someday, perhaps, he too will be one of us. If you can lead him to our side, he would be yours. And the two of you could rule Magnus together. Is that enough of an end for you?"

She didn't answer. She gave the beggar a small coin.

"Go then," the beggar said, bobbing his head in pretended gratitude. "I need not tell you how to win a man. But be careful of your own heart. If he won't come to our side, the trust you gain will be necessary for us to end his life."

Just as Thomas began to make out the jumble of vats and clay pots in the dimness of the candle maker's shop, a ghostlike bundle of dirty white cloth rose from a corner and moved toward him.

Thomas brought up his fists in protection, then relaxed as he noticed that the worn shoes at the base of the ghost had very human toes poking through the leather.

He backed away to make room, and the bundle of cloth scurried past, bumping him with a solidness that no ghost possessed. Moments later, it squeezed past Tiny John.

Isabelle stepped into the shop, making Thomas realize she'd slipped away for a few moments, but he didn't give her short absence any more thought.

"That's Katherine," Geoffrey said to Thomas. "Daughter of the previous candle maker. Ignore her. She's surprised because I've returned early from the market, and she's afraid of people."

Thomas watched her shuffle past a curtain and out of sight into the back of the cramped house.

"The bandages around her head?" William asked.

"It's to keep people from screaming at the sight of *her*. When she was little—I am told—she reached up and grabbed a pot of hot wax. No mind that she'd been warned a hundred times. No mind at all. She learned the lesson, she did. The foolish child jumped blind into the flame warming the pot. As bright as a torch she became. The business that was lost because of her screaming." The candle maker waved his hands, dismissing the girl's pain. "It's a curse she did not die. I was stuck with her as part of the arrangement to take over this shop on the owner's death. Who might marry her now?" The candle maker shrugged. "The will of the Lord, I suppose."

Year after year at the abbey compressed into a single moment for Thomas. He turned on the candle maker with a bitterness he did not know he possessed. "How can you say there is a God who permits this? How can you give that girl less pity than a dog?"

"Thomas." William's calm rebuke drew Thomas from his sudden emotion.

"I give her a home," the candle maker said in a hurried voice. "It's much more than any dog gets."

Thomas told himself he had no right to interfere. "I ask your forgiveness," he said coldly and without a trace of apology. "For a moment, her situation reminded me of someone I once knew."

Thomas's heart cried for the pain he knew the candle maker's daughter had suffered; yet moments later, his brain sadly told him there was no use in caring. In this town alone, there were dozens of beggars and cripples who had less than Katherine.

I guess, Thomas added silently to himself, *that evidence of pain is all the more reason to be angry at this God those false monks so often proclaimed.*

Thomas changed the subject. "We came for candles."

Relief brightened the candle maker's face. "Yes. I'll bring my finest."

He clapped his hands twice. Immediately Katherine appeared with a wooden box.

"She must earn her keep," Geoffrey said defensively as he glanced at Thomas.

Thomas said nothing. He looked away from the bundle of cloth with outstretched arms. The wrap around Katherine's head was stained with age, almost caked black around the hole slashed open for her mouth.

"These are my best candles," Geoffrey said.

"Perhaps these are the best candles you have. But compared to London…" William shook his head.

"I've not been to London," Geoffrey said, wistfulness apparent in his voice. "Few of us ever leave Magnus." He coughed quickly to hide embarrassment at his ignorance, then grabbed the box from Katherine and shook his head as she cowered and waited for instructions.

Thomas felt a hand on his shoulder, even as he winced to see Katherine's fear. Isabelle had moved close to him. Tiny John seemed subdued at the horror of Katherine's primitive mask and clung to the edges of Isabelle's dress. The three of them stood in a tight cluster, and Thomas felt a great sadness to know their instinctive joining resulted from their shared status of outcast. At the same time, he felt warmth to be part of this makeshift family.

"I apprenticed with the best master for miles around," Geoffrey said. "I don't need to see London candles to know these burn as bright as any in the land."

"A farthing each dozen," William offered. "If the candles are as good as any to be found, what of the rest of Magnus? Is it the horrible place it is rumored to be?"

"Two farthings and no lower," Geoffrey countered. "And strangers as good as you have said less about Magnus and died for it."

Thomas gave the conversation his full attention.

"Two farthings for a dozen and a half." William lowered his voice. "And who might be doing the killing?"

Geoffrey shook his head and held out his hand. "The color of your money first. This box holds three dozen candles."

"Four farthings, then. You drive a hard bargain." William counted the coins. "About this fearsome domain…"

Even in the dimness of the shop, Thomas could see the eager glint of a born gossip in the candle maker's eyes.

"A fearsome domain indeed," Geoffrey said. He looked around his shop, as though searching for eavesdroppers. "Ever since Richard Mewburn disposed of the proper lord."

"Surely the Earl of York would not permit such an unlawful occurrence as murder within his realm."

"Bah." Geoffrey waved his pudgy fingers. "That happened twenty years ago. Since then, murder is the least of evils here in Magnus. The slightest of crimes results in hideous punishment. Men with their ankles crushed for failing to bow to Richard's sheriff. Branded faces for holding back crops—even though the poor are taxed almost to starvation." Geoffrey lowered his voice. "The Earl of York is paid rich tribute to stay away. It is whispered that some evil blackmail prevented the earl's father from dispensing justice after Magnus was taken by force, blackmail that still holds the current earl long after the father's death from—"

Katherine gasped. She had not moved since delivering the candles. The first sound of her voice, eerie and muffled from behind the swath of dirty rags around her head, startled Thomas.

"You cannot reveal this to strangers," she protested. "It is enough to sentence them to death!"

Geoffrey brought his hand up quickly, as if to strike her. She stepped back and bumped a table. Two clay candle molds teetered, then fell to the ground and smashed into dust.

"Clumsy wretch!" the candle maker snarled. He grabbed a thin willow stick from the table beside him and whipped it across the side of her head.

Had Thomas paused to think, he would have decided it was her complete acceptance of the pain that drove him to action. She did not cry, did not whimper, merely bowed her head and waited for the next blow.

The animal had struck her face. What more cruel reminder of her deformity could exist?

Holy rage burst inside Thomas.

The candle maker raised his arm to strike again. Thomas roared and dove across the narrow space between them. He crashed full force into the candle maker, and they both fell to the ground. Before the candle maker could react, Thomas pounced on his chest.

Fury possessed Thomas and he grabbed Geoffrey by both ears. He pulled the candle maker's head inches from the floor and held it. His arms shook as he fought an overpowering urge to dash the candle maker's head against the stone in one savage motion.

"Foul, horrid creature," ground Thomas between clenched teeth. "You shall pay dearly for the abuse—"

He did not finish his threat.

William pulled him upward, and during that motion, soldiers burst into the shop.

Had William not been so helpless with both his arms around Thomas, he might have been able to reach between his shoulder blades and pull the sword free from where it had been strapped in a sheath on his back.

Instead, less than a second later, three soldiers had him pinned against the wall. Two other soldiers grabbed Thomas.

"You hail from the abbey at Harland Moor," one of the soldiers holding Thomas said. It was not a question. "Three monks have been found dead there. One by a blow to the head. Two by poisoning." The soldier grinned. "You and your large companion here will hang. You for murder. Your companion for aiding a murderer in escape."

TWENTY-ONE

Late morning heat baked the bandages that covered Katherine's face. In heat like this, it always seemed that she could not draw enough air, no matter how she strained her lungs. Yet it was more than the heat outside that made her long for the cool shadows of the candle shop. She hated crowds. She hated the mockery and taunting of children; she hated the unexpected jostling, for the small holes left for her eyes gave her little vision, and most sounds that reached her were muffled and displaced.

So she walked with hesitation through the marketplace, holding her basket as close to her side as possible, and hoping Hawkwood might find her soon.

"Fresh bread! Fresh bread!"

Katherine turned her head to seek the source of the cries.

No. It wasn't Hawkwood. This seller of bread was a man with only one arm. The other arm, ending at his elbow, tucked a long loaf of bread against his ribs. Hawkwood was a master of altered appearances, but even he could not give the illusion of a stumped arm.

"Potions! Healing potions! Love potions!"

Katherine turned her head in the opposite direction. An old woman, face half-hidden in the shadows of a bonnet, leaned over a rough table covered with dried herbs. Inside her bandage, Katherine smiled. Hawkwood would enjoy the irony of posing as someone with knowledge of herbs and potions.

Katherine moved closer to the old woman and pretended to scan the table.

"Potions!" the old woman screamed again to be heard above the din of the market. "Healing potions! Love potions!"

Katherine waited. Would Hawkwood give her the phrase?

"Scat, girl," the old woman hissed. "You'll turn others away. I've nothing to restore a face like yours."

Katherine hesitated. There might be someone standing right behind, unseen to her, and Hawkwood had no choice but to react thus.

"Scat! Scat!" The woman's voice rose to a strained screech. "No love potion would earn you even a blind fool!"

Katherine backed away. What was it in the weak and the hurt, so far from nobility, that took satisfaction in showing cruelty to those even weaker and more hurt?

Something bumped her ankle. It was awkward, bending over so far that she might be able to see the ground through the eyeholes of her bandage.

The object at her feet was a red ball.

Before she could puzzle further, a second ball, blue, rolled past the red one. Then a green ball.

"Ho, ho, fair lady! A tiny farthing is all I require." A man danced in front of her, scooped the balls into his hands, and began to juggle. "One farthing and laughter is yours."

Katherine shook her head. Whatever reason Hawkwood had for arranging the three lit candles at the altar of the church to wait her morning prayers, it was important enough to have summoned her forth. She could not dally, not even for a jester with a bouncy, belled hat, twinkling eyes, painted face, and ridiculous red and green tights.

The jester spun the balls in a tighter circle so that they were almost a blur. Blue, red, green. "Come, come, fair lady. The Lord loves laughter. Heaven stands open at the sound!"

Heaven stands open.

Katherine did laugh. Again, Hawkwood had managed to arrive unexpectedly. "One farthing, then. For when heaven stands open, only fools turn away."

Hawkwood nodded, satisfied from her answer that it was indeed her beneath the bandages. They both knew that should she ever be discovered, two things were certain. Her death, and then someone put in her place behind the bandages for the very purpose of capturing Hawkwood.

"Arrange to deliver candles to Gervaise," he said in a lowered voice. "I shall be in the church when the midafternoon bells ring."

Katherine set down her basket and clapped as his juggling continued. Appearances might be important.

The jester bowed, then reached into a bag at his feet and pulled out a short, straight stick. He tilted his head back and balanced the stick on his chin. He began to juggle again, stick tottering, as he walked away from Katherine to cajole attention from others in the marketplace.

The stone walls of the church provided cool air, and as Katherine entered, she stopped to set down the cloth bag of candles. She pulled her clothes away from her body and flapped them to enjoy the relief of that air against hot and sticky skin.

"Welcome, Katherine." The words greeted her from the shadows of a large pillar. "I trust these candles are of the same fine quality that our father priest has come to expect."

"Yes, Gervaise," she answered as her eyes adjusted to the dimness. "Geoffrey complains, of course, that for what payment he receives, he should call the candles a contribution of charity."

Gervaise was an elderly man with gray hair combed straight back. A plain cassock covered his slight body, and he stood with his hands in front of him, folded together. "Please, Katherine, let me help you with that bundle."

"Thank you," she said.

As he stooped to take the candles, he said, "Will you bring these to the nave? I'll set the others in storage."

Again Katherine nodded. The elaborate acting, she felt, was rarely necessary, but Hawkwood insisted they always behave as if enemy ears were nearby and open. He said the island of Magnus was riddled with enough hidden passages that those ears could very well be there.

In the nave she began to remove from the candelabra the stubs of burnt candles to replace them with new. Not for the first time did it anger her to see the finely wrought gold of the candelabrum gleaming in the light that poured in through stained glass high above. How many mouths could this gold feed; how fat must the clergy become?

Something bumped her ankle and rolled over her foot. A red ball.

She smiled, a movement that scraped her skin against the tight bandages. When she turned, she saw the outline of a figure in the shadows behind the beam of light. Wordlessly, she moved closer.

She saw Hawkwood as he usually was. An old man, bent beneath a black cape.

"M'lord," she whispered, "fare thee well, here where heaven stands open for those who believe?"

Hawkwood relaxed at the familiar words and pressed farther back so that he stood in a recess of the wall, invisible in deep shadow. Katherine moved in front of him and bowed her head. Any unexpected visitor would see only her, deep in meditation.

"Katherine, I fare well. Magnus, however, may not."

"M'lord?"

"In the candle shop, you were visited yesterday by two men, each now in the dungeons."

"Yes. They were strangely familiar."

He nodded. "The older is one of us. A knight and a good friend of mine."

Katherine drew in a startled breath, loud enough in the cool silence of the inner sanctum of the church that it echoed from the far walls.

"The other," Hawkwood continued, "is one I had hoped long ago might take Magnus from the enemy."

"Then if we release them from the dungeon…," Katherine began.

"We must, yet the knight is well known to the enemy," Hawkwood said. "He fought hard when Magnus fell all those years ago and was barely able to escape with his life. We must find a way to let them escape without revealing how we have hidden ourselves in their presence all these years."

"If he is well known to them, why did he return to certain death?"

"Because of the other," Hawkwood replied. He took a moment to gather his thoughts. Katherine did not interrupt. She rarely did. "The one named Thomas. We play a terrible cat-and-mouse game with the enemy." Katherine could not see his grim smile, but she heard it in his voice. "And we are the mouse. They know, as do we, the knight's purpose here. They can afford to let him live while the rest of the game is played. What we do not know is the heart of the other, Thomas."

"Thomas? He is a good man," Katherine said quickly. Too quickly.

"Katherine," Hawkwood said gently, "do not let his countenance sway you."

She stiffened. "Hardly. Do I forsake what little teaching I have received?"

"My apologies."

"He defended me," she said. "A man comely enough that he could choose among maidens fought for a freak behind bandages. What says that of his heart?"

"Would that I could believe it," Hawkwood said, "for in this cat-and-mouse game, none could suspect that you are one of us, placed in the candle maker's shop since childhood. Thomas, then, had no other reason to defend you than what lay in his heart."

"He, too, is part of this terrible game?"

"Yes, Katherine. As you were hidden here, so was Thomas hidden in an abbey. I've just now discovered, by the accusations against him, that it was the abbey at Harland Moor. That may help us soon, but I'm not certain of it. We'll need to send someone there to learn more about his boyhood. Complicating things, he has been accused of the monks' murder."

"I never believed he murdered them!"

"Is that your heart speaking? Or your mind?"

She didn't answer.

"Beware of listening too closely to your heart. You must acknowledge that he fled the abbey in suspicious circumstances. One monk is dead from a blow to the head. Two others poisoned. The survivor testifies that Thomas is responsible. Until we know the truth about that too, we must proceed as if he cannot be trusted, even though he was to be taught in our ways and given the way to take Magnus."

"Was?" Katherine said.

Hawkwood smiled at her back. "You have wisdom beyond your years. In happier times, you would already be the best of a new generation of Immortals."

"He is not one of us?"

Hawkwood said, "The one who was to teach him died too soon. We do not know what happened in the years since. He appeared at the gallows to rescue the knight, but I fear he was sent by our enemy in hopes that we would trust him completely."

"Yet," Katherine said, "he may *not* be the enemy."

"Is it hope that you express?"

She said nothing.

"Yes, Katherine, he may not be the enemy. And if he acts on his own, he needs our help until we are certain he can be trusted."

"If he acts on his own, he knows nothing of us or of them," she protested. "It is like sending a sheep into battle against ravenous wolves."

"This, too, I have considered," Hawkwood said. "Yet who shall we risk to deliver the knowledge? For the enemy still searches, and if he is one of them, the deliverer is doomed. We are so few that we can spare none."

Katherine sighed. "Yes m'lord."

"However," Hawkwood said, "it does not mean we shall abandon him or the knight completely. It is fortunate indeed that Thomas defended you as he did."

"M'lord?"

"You now have ample reason to befriend him."

I ailer!" William shouted at the rusted iron door. He did not expect an answer. "Two days have passed. Surely the lord of this manor must appear to us soon!"

"Shhh!" hissed the man who hunched in the corner of the cell. He pointed at a tiny hole.

William groaned and looked to Thomas for sympathy.

Thomas shrugged and grinned. Under the circumstances—their fellow prisoner had said nothing since they had been flung into the cell—there was little else to do.

What light appeared in the cell came from oily torches outside the grated opening in the door. It took Thomas only two large steps to cross the space between the clammy stone walls, three steps to cover front and back. It was so cramped that had the fetters on the walls been used, one from each side could have placed their wrists in manacles. Yet there were three of them in this small space, sharing the bedding of trampled straw that soaked up the wet dungeon filth.

Thomas dug inside his shirt, searched quickly with his fingers, and snorted in triumph. "Found it."

He withdrew his hand and squeezed the flea between the nails of his thumb and forefinger until he felt a tiny snap.

"Spare me the battle glories, Thomas," William said. "We have much greater concerns. If we are able to meet the lord of this manor, we can present our case. He will see there is no injustice in the fate of those monks and then release us."

"I regret not sending that letter to the mother abbey at Rievaulx," Thomas said almost absently as he scratched himself. "We might have been spared this."

William did not have to ask which letter. In the two endless days of darkness and solitude—interrupted only by the bowls of porridge shoved between the bars twice daily—Thomas had told the knight of his final day at the abbey, including the letter of evidence against the monks.

"How often must I tell you?" William said with gentleness. "Unless the lord of Magnus learns who truly did poison them, we will hang. He must appear to accuse us so that we can defend ourselves." Then the knight grinned. "As I've also told you many times since our arrest, there is justice in the monks poisoning themselves."

Thomas grinned back but without much feeling. It gave him little consolation that he had guessed right in his final hour at the abbey. As he had done countless times during the slow passage of time in the dungeon cell, Thomas replayed in his mind the moments before Monk Walter had lashed out with a heavy fist...

"Quit your blathering," Monk Walter said between clenched teeth. *"Send the boy on his way. Now!"*

Monk Philip clamped his jaw as if coming to a decision. *"Not to his death. Nor shall I go meet God without attempting some good."* He drew a lungful of air. *"Thomas, leave alone the—"*

Leave alone the *food,* Thomas had realized as Monk Philip died. It could be nothing else. The monks knew Thomas would immediately retrieve the letter of condemnation upon leaving the abbey. By inserting a slow-acting poison into his requested provisions, he would die later and never reveal their crimes.

Yet he could only speculate at the rest, based on the descriptions of the monks who had died. Philip, of course, had died from hitting his head after Monk Walter tried to stop him from revealing the food was poisoned. Prior Jack and Monk Frederick were the other bodies. With Thomas gone and the other two aware of his witchcraft, Monk Walter's life was a stake. If Prior Jack and Monk Frederick revealed this to anyone, Monk Walter would be tried and executed. As a practitioner familiar with potions, Monk Walter had skills with poison. He could have easily administered doses of poison to Prior Jack and Monk Frederick, the same kind of poison they'd planned for Thomas's death. Monk Walter, no doubt, had decided if Thomas wasn't dead, the others must be silenced by poison.

"The lord of Magnus will never appear," crowed the man in the corner.

"Ho, ho! After two days, the man of silence speaks," William observed. "Have you tired of your scavenging friends?"

"My good fellow, in my time here, I have seen many like you come, then go to the hangman," the man said, apparently unperturbed by William's jesting tone. "I learned early not to befriend any. It proves to be too disappointing." He gestured at the corner hole with his hands. "These furry creatures that make their visits, however, are not so fickle. They require little food and their gratitude is quite rewarding. And *they* always return."

Thomas shuddered. He hoped he would not remain so long in the cell that rats would be more attractive than human company. Not when he had the means to conquer Magnus. *If only I could escape—all it would take is one clear night and...*

The man dusted his hands of the last of the breadcrumbs he had patiently held in front of the hole, breadcrumbs saved from the occasional time that more was given than just porridge.

"You said the lord of Magnus would never appear," Thomas prompted.

The man did not rise from his squatting position. He merely swiveled on the balls of his feet to face them. His cheeks were rounded like those of a well-stuffed chipmunk. Ears thick and almost flappy. Half-balding forehead, and shaggy hair that fell from the back of his head to well below his shoulders. Patched clothing as filthy as the straw that clung to his matted and exposed chest hair.

"It is time to introduce myself," he said with a lopsided grin that showed strong teeth. "My name is Waleran." He stood, shuffled forward, and extended his empty right hand in the traditional clasp that symbolized a lack of weapons. "Generally visitors hear nothing from me," he said after William and Thomas had shaken hands with him. "Unlike you, they arrive alone and learn to ignore me after several days. Thus, I am allowed my peace. With two of you, however, the constant talking has given me little peace, and finally I am driven to break my silence."

"Two days of waiting shows remarkable patience," William said.

Waleran shrugged. "I have been here ten years. Time means nothing."

Water ticked in a constant drip from the roof of the dungeon cell to the floor.

"Ten years!" Thomas examined him again. Although pale, Waleran seemed in good health.

"You wonder what crime sends a man here?" Waleran replied to Thomas's frank stare. "Simply the crime of being a villager in Magnus.

My son, you see, went to the fields outside the castle one harvest day. Instead of threshing grain, he departed. London, perhaps. I am held here as hostage until he returns. And I am held as an example. As long as I am here, other families know the lord is serious in his edict. No man, woman, or child may leave the village except to work in the fields and return before nightfall."

"That's monstrous!"

Waleran smiled wanly at Thomas. "Indeed. But who is to defy the lord?"

William began pacing the cell. "It is a strange manor, this Magnus. The lord murders its rightful owner, yet the Earl of York does not interfere. Entire families are kept virtual prisoners inside the castle walls, yet the village does not resist."

"Strange, perhaps, but understandable," Waleran said quietly. "You've seen the fortifications of the castle and outside walls. Even a man as powerful as the Earl of York knows it is fruitless to attack. Besides, the lord of this manor is shrewd enough to give no cause for the earl's anger."

William raised an eyebrow.

"Because the entire village is in vassalage, this manor is extremely wealthy. The lord gives ample homage to the Earl of York in the form of grain, wool, and even gold. Simple, don't you see?"

"I do see," William said thoughtfully. "The Earl of York is bribed not to attack a castle in his kingdom, which he could not successfully overcome anyway."

"Yes, yes!" Waleran nodded quickly. "And with enough soldiers within the gates, the villagers are powerless. Those who do leave to till and harvest the fields know they must return each night, or family members will be placed in these very cells. Richard Mewburn as lord of

Magnus may be well hated by those inside Magnus, but all are helpless before him."

"What I don't see," William said in the same thoughtful tone, "is why this lord has not appeared to formally accuse us. We deserve the justice that must be granted anywhere in the land."

Waleran only shook his head. He returned to his corner, found a crumb to hold above the rat hole, and squatted in his former position. Minutes passed, broken only by the never-ending drips of water onto the stone.

Thomas could not stand it any longer. "That is all?" he cried. "You are choosing silence again?"

Waleran slowly craned his head upward and measured his words. "My silence would be better for you." He sighed heavily. "Remember I am a reluctant messenger."

Thomas thought of the empty road leading into Magnus. He remembered the stories Isabelle and William had already told. Strong premonition told him he did not want to hear Waleran's next words.

"Magnus has around it a black silence," Waleran said. "Traders and craftsmen learned long ago that they risked freedom and all they owned to visit. Whispers of death keep them away. And for good reason."

Waleran looked back to the hole and spoke as if addressing the wall. "Had there not been convenient charges against you, you would still have found yourselves within this dungeon. There are dark secrets in Magnus. Secrets that must remain hidden from the entire land."

He paused, and the deadness in his voice spoke chilling truth. "Why would the lord appear to hear your case? He needn't bother, for the truth is simple. Strangers, once inside these walls, are never permitted to leave."

TWENTY-THREE

T homas woke with the sour taste of heavy sleep in his mouth. He rolled into a sitting position and wiped straw from his face.

How is a person to mark the passage of time in this dark hole? he muttered in his mind. *No bells to mark the church offices; no sun to mark dawn or nightfall.*

In the unending flickering of torches, Thomas could see that Waleran lay huddled motionless on one side of the cell; William snored gently in his corner.

The knight is tired too, Thomas observed.

Because he knew the boredom that stretched ahead, Thomas concentrated on a routine to delay his restlessness. He plucked from his mind the first of many well-worn questions, determined to gnaw it yet again, like an animal searching for the tiniest shred of undiscovered meat.

It demanded patience to turn first one question, then another, over and over in his mind, to approach it from every angle, to fit different facts into place. In four days of captivity, Thomas had concluded nothing new from all his questions and thoughts. However, all he had was time, and the questions, like him, would not leave the cell.

Who is this knight? Thomas asked himself. *A man of honor, he fulfilled his pledge by entering the castle walls of Magnus. He has become a friend, yet he speaks nothing of his past, nothing of his own quest.*

Regardless of his past, he, like any knight, no doubt could easily defeat a dozen unarmed and untrained peasants. But William no longer had a sword or chain mail, for he had been searched before being thrown into the dungeon, with loud, angry questions about how the objects had come into his possession, questions William answered by saying he'd stolen them.

Thomas, in his well-rehearsed routine, moved to the next question. What would happen to Tiny John and Isabelle?

Tiny John, no doubt, could well find a way to survive. But was Isabelle withstanding the terrors of being alone and friendless in Magnus? Thomas let worry fill his hunger-pinched stomach. And guilt, remembering how she'd protested the journey to Magnus and how she'd predicted the worst would happen. What work would she find to sustain her? What stranger might treat her with kindness? Or—Thomas dreaded the thought—would she simply flee Magnus and disappear from his life forever?

Thomas smiled at his own foolishness. Logic told him that—barring a miracle—he and the knight would never leave this cell for anything but death by hanging. Worrying about a future with a girl should not even be a concern.

Thomas moved to his next question.

He closed his eyes and pictured himself in the panicked darkness in front of the scaffold less than a week earlier. Again and again, Thomas replayed those few minutes of terror beneath a blackened sky. The old man had known it was Thomas beneath those robes. The old man had known how Thomas had given the illusions of power. And the old man had known of his desire to win Magnus.

How had that mysterious old man known so much? Who was the

old man? And what had Sarah meant about the Immortals? Would he find out here in Magnus?

And then there was the question of escape. Thomas's power came from prepared potions and other trickery he could manage as if it were magic. He had none now, for he'd carefully hidden everything in his sacks outside Magnus before entering. And William had no weapons.

It appeared the two of them were helpless, but surely he could think of some kind of solution, couldn't he? Thomas attacked that problem with such intensity that William had to clap his hands to get his attention.

"Thomas, you scowl as if we have lost all hope."

Thomas blinked himself free from his trance and answered the knight's easy smile. "Never!" Although it felt like a hollow promise.

William yawned. "My mouth is as vile as goat's dung. Even the water from this roof will be better."

The knight moved beneath one of the eternal drips and opened his mouth wide. After several patient minutes of collecting water, he rinsed and spit into a far corner of the cell.

Waleran unfolded from his motionless huddle and grumbled, "Must you be so noisy? My friends will never venture forth."

William merely yawned again and said, "Precisely."

Before Waleran could retort, the door rattled.

"A visitor," droned the jailer.

"Impossible," Waleran said. "Not once in ten years has a visitor been permitted to—"

The door lurched open, and the jailer's hand appeared briefly as he pushed a stumbling figure inside. Thomas tried not to stare. Caked and dirty bandages still suggested mutilated horror. A downcast head and dropped shoulders still projected fear.

Katherine. In one hand, she held a candle on a holder, the flame barely casting any light in the dimness of the cell. In her other hand, she gripped the handle of a basket.

"Who is this wretched creature?" Waleran demanded.

Thomas spun, shoved his palm into Waleran's chest and drove him backward into the filth.

"Another word and you shall pay—," Thomas began in a low, tight voice.

William stepped between them. "Thomas…"

Thomas sucked air between gritted teeth to calm himself as Waleran scrabbled backward into his corner.

"Please do not hurt him," Katherine said clearly. "To be called 'wretched creature' is an insult only if I choose to believe it."

Thomas turned to her. She had set down her basket and candle holder and stood waiting, hands behind her back. She was only slightly shorter than he. Her voice, still muffled by the swathed bandages, had a low sweetness.

"I beg your pardon," Thomas said. It pained him to look at her. Not because she was a freak, but because he remembered his own pain and loneliness. It tore at his heart to imagine how much worse she felt her private agony.

"How is it you are allowed to visit?" William asked.

Katherine's head dipped in shyness. "Every day since your capture, I have brought hot meals to the captain of the guards. I have washed his laundry, cleaned his rooms."

"Bribery!" William laughed. "But why?"

Katherine knelt and set the basket on the floor. "Because of the candle shop. Not once has a person defended me as you both did," she answered. "Prisoners here do not fare well. I wished to comfort you."

Still kneeling, she pulled away the cloth that covered the basket. The light of the candle showed bread. Apples. Chicken. Cheese.

"These luxuries are more than you can afford," Thomas protested.

"Please," she said, setting the candle holder beside the basket. "Rarely am I treated with kindness. And rarely am I able to return a kindness. This is what I want to do."

"Thank you," Thomas said. Refusing would rob her of dignity.

"I have little time," Katherine said. "If it pleases you, Thomas, I wish to speak privately."

The jail cell was so small that to accomplish it, she backed up to the cell door, and Thomas had to step within inches of her and whisper lightly enough to keep the sound from going more than a few feet.

"You know my name," Thomas said.

"Your friend Tiny John told me."

"Tiny John! He is well?"

"As long as he continues to avoid the soldiers." He had to strain to hear the softness of her voice. "Many of the shopkeepers take delight in helping that rascal. They like to see the soldiers made fools of."

Thomas pictured Tiny John darting from hiding spot to hiding spot, never losing his grin. "And the girl?"

Katherine drew a quick breath and turned her head away as she spoke. "The girl truly is beautiful. And you are very handsome. I understand your concern."

Thomas silently cursed himself. Here she stood, knowing her hideous face prevented her from competing for more affection. And while she waited, with the only gifts she could afford, the passing stranger betrayed such obvious concern for another with beauty she would never have. *Thoughtless cruelty of the worst type.*

Katherine faced him squarely again, but her voice trembled as she whispered. "She has disappeared. But if you ask, I shall inquire for you and search until she is found."

"No. Please do not look for her." He blocked thoughts of Isabelle and measured his words carefully. "We might ask instead that you honor us with another visit."

The squaring of her shoulders told him he had answered correctly.

Besides, he consoled himself, even if Katherine found Isabelle, what good would it accomplish?

The jailer rapped on the door. "Be quick about leaving."

"Tomorrow," Katherine whispered, taking his hands, "we shall talk of escape."

"Escape?" he whispered.

She pressed a piece of paper into his palm. He closed his fingers on it.

"Step backward," she said.

Puzzled, he obeyed. His heel hit the basket. As he glanced down, he noticed that she nudged the candle with her foot. It toppled into the straw on the floor, and flames immediately leapt upward.

Waleran shouted warning. The knight jumped to his feet.

Katherine kicked at the straw and the flames spread.

As Waleran darted forward to stomp out the flames, she took advantage of the distraction and pressed herself against Thomas, pulling a short sword from beneath her dirty shawl.

In a flash, he understood and slipped it beneath his own shirt. He stomped the remaining flames out alongside Waleran and the knight.

"You stupid, stupid girl!" Waleran shouted, whirling toward Katherine. "That could have been the death of us."

"Treat her with respect!" Thomas stepped between them, and the man retreated.

Thomas turned to say good-bye to Katherine, but she had already backed away to the cell door, and the guard was roughly pulling her outside, cursing her for the smoky accident.

Later, when Waleran was on his side and sleeping with his face to the far wall, Thomas opened the slip of paper that Katherine had given him.

He thought it was strange that she assumed he could read. Equally strange that she could read. And even more strange, the contents of the note.

You will find paper and quill hidden beneath the food to allow us to plan escape. Be cautious of what you say in front of the other prisoner. I learned from the guards he was brought into this prison only hours before you arrived.

Twenty-Four

Hours later, Thomas stared at the ceiling of the dungeon cell, deep in thought. He'd been given a weapon. But how could it help?

Part of his mind idly noted each new drop of falling water. *Water.* Thomas swallowed and licked dry lips. *Water.* He remembered how each morning the sour taste of sleep seemed so peculiar. *Water.* A new realization startled him.

He ran idea after idea through his mind. Then, much later, he spoke.

"Escape!" he whispered hoarsely. "I know how we can escape!"

On his back, eyes closed, William muttered, "Let me sleep. It's the only escape I have."

"Escape!" Thomas said again.

Waleran stirred from his patient perch near the hole where rats fled. "What's that you say?"

Thomas grinned at Waleran in response, then stepped across the dungeon cell and shook the knight. "Escape!" He looked over to Waleran. "Yes! I said *escape*! I think I have an idea."

"Lad, you've become delusional," William said. "Tell me how you got there. I'd like to join you."

"Not a delusion." Thomas grinned at Waleran, then at the knight. "I have decided many things. One is this." He paused and took a deep breath. "William, I need you to trust me completely. I need that trust to ensure our escape plans will not fail."

William nodded.

"Katherine will return. She made that promise. I will give her a message with instructions for John to retrieve the gold and give her enough to bribe the captain of the guards to leave the door unlocked." Thomas paused. "We will need on that day the excellence of a knight who can fight as no other."

William warned Thomas with a glance. "Where do we find such a knight?"

"Trust me." Thomas added urgency to his voice. "Pledge your fighting skills on my behalf and you will be rewarded with the gold I have already earned."

"You have me thoroughly puzzled, Thomas," William said, giving a warning glance to indicate Thomas should shut his mouth in front of Waleran. "I have no skills to demonstrate. The sword and chain mail I stole from a knight."

Thomas ignored the warning in William's voice. "Come, come." He laughed. "Such modesty." He grinned again at Waleran. "He *is* a knight."

Waleran's jaw dropped. So did William's. Each, Thomas had no doubt, for a different reason.

"Yes. A knight!" Thomas said. "Something no other person in Magnus knows. And his fighting skills will lead us to safety." He gestured impatiently at William. "Please. Impress us with your swordplay."

"You are a fool," William growled. He lurched to his feet and wiped sleep from his eyes. "There is no sword in this prison cell." He yawned and shook himself awake, much as a dog shakes water.

"No?" Thomas pulled the short sword Katherine had given him from his shirt and handed it to William.

Waleran gaped at the sight.

"Yours," Thomas said to William. "Hide it in the straw until the day we need it."

"You cannot believe in God. Not if you tell me He is a God of love," Thomas insisted in a low voice.

"Why is that?" Katherine replied calmly.

Thomas welcomed the sound of her voice. Katherine's sweetness banished the darkness. With every visit each morning since Katherine had first walked into the cell, Thomas learned how her voice was so expressive that he did not need to read her face to enjoy their discussions. He hardly noticed the bandages around her head. Moreover, her presence gave such gentle calmness that he wanted to speak of things he had shared with no living soul since the death of Sarah.

"It is hard to believe," he said, "when there is so much evidence that your God does not love anyone."

They did not talk of escape, because whenever she held his hand to bid hello upon entering the cell, they exchanged notes of paper to plan escape. Later, he'd decided, he would ask the questions that burned. How was it she could read? How did she know he could read?

"Nothing in my life," he continued with intensity, "shows such a God. My parents were taken from me—killed by pestilence—before I was old enough to remember them. Then Sarah—my nurse, teacher, and only friend—gone before I was eleven years of age." Thomas struggled to keep his fists unclenched. "Surely if this God of yours existed,

He would have been there in the abbey when all human love failed me. He was not. Instead, there was only corruption by the very men pretending to serve Him."

He described his years in the abbey and the crimes of the four monks.

"And outside of the abbey," he continued, "a land where most people struggle to live day by day, servants to the very few and very wealthy earls and lords. Beggars, cripples, disease, and death. There is nothing good in this life."

"Thomas, Thomas..." Katherine placed a cool hand upon his.

He shook free. "And you," he blurted with anger. "How could you be so cursed if God truly loved...?" Then he realized what he was saying. "I'm sorry," he said in a low voice.

"Do not trouble yourself," Katherine said. "I am accustomed to the covering of my face." She touched her bandages lightly. "This is not a curse. It is only a burden. After all, our time on earth is so short. And God is more interested in our hearts and souls than in our appearances."

She moved her hand away from her face and held it up to stop Thomas from protesting. "Think of a magnificent carpet, Thomas. Thousands and thousands of threads intertwined in a beautiful pattern. No single thread can comprehend the pattern. No single thread can see its purpose. Yet together, they make the glorious entirety." She continued with controlled passion. "You and I are threads, Thomas. We cannot see God's plan for us. My scars, your loneliness, the beggars' hunger, and the paths of men in war and peace all lead to the completion of God's design."

"How do you know with such certainty?"

"God grants you peace when you accept Him."

Thomas shook his head slowly. "I wish I could believe." His voice rose with passion. "When I left the abbey, I left all pretensions to God. I shall not return."

His statement left a silence between them.

On the other side of the dungeon, William sat in a slouched position, ignoring them. Waleran squatted and waited with breadcrumbs for the rats to visit.

The silence between them nearly became uncomfortable. Thomas decided to ask the question he had delayed from fear.

"Tiny John. Did he succeed?"

"Yes, Thomas. I have made the arrangements."

Gratitude swept across him, warming him against the chill of the cell. For the first time since her visits began, she replaced in his heart, for a moment, Isabelle's beautiful face and haunting eyes.

"Then it is nearly time," he murmured. "Spread the legend among the villagers."

Katherine nodded. "When is it," she murmured in return, "that you wish to escape?"

"In six days," Thomas said. "On the eve of the sixth day from now."

TWENTY-FIVE

When the jailer opened the door to send in a visitor, Thomas expected to see Katherine.

Instead, it was Isabelle.

He felt the quickening of his heart.

When she extended a hand toward him, he stood from where he'd been sitting in the straw and moved away from William and Waleran. He allowed her to lead him into the far corner, and she moved close to him, standing on her toes to put her face close to his.

"Thomas," she said. "I have deceived you. I hope you can forgive me."

"I trust you had good reason."

The cell was so small that at all times the dripping of the water could be plainly heard. Thomas guessed that William and Waleran could overhear every word above a whisper. He hardly cared—it felt so good to see Isabelle.

"Deception was my protection," she said. "I have secrets and need to stay hidden from pursuers." She held both his hands and continued to transfix him with a deep gaze. "Perhaps you will protect me?"

"I am in prison." But he smiled, showing confidence, not fear.

"You are capable of much," she said. "I know this. You will escape."

"Who are your pursuers?" he asked.

She squeezed his hands and leaned forward to kiss his cheek. Then she stepped back and watched him. "Trust me. When the time is right, I will tell you everything."

Slowly, he nodded.

He had much more to ask, but the guard interrupted by opening the door and informing them that the girl had been given all the time she'd paid for.

With a final soft kiss on his cheek, she walked away.

Isabelle, he thought, touching his cheek. *Isabelle.*

Thomas recognized the voice echoing in the dungeon hallways long before he could understand the words.

William stopped his silent pacing. "That's—"

"Our pickpocket friend," Thomas finished.

The knight squinted and opened his mouth to ask a question but was interrupted by the clanging of a key in the cell door.

"Horrid fiend!" the guard shouted. "I hope they tear you into pieces!"

A bleeding hand shoved Tiny John into the cell. He stumbled but did not fall. The door slammed shut.

Tiny John surveyed his new home with his hands on his hips and grinned. "Barely nicked him, I did," he explained. "If only my teeth were bigger, I'd have bitten those fingers clean through."

William shook his head in mock disgust.

Waleran moved closer, not bothering to hide a puzzled expression. "Who are you? And what did that soldier mean, 'I hope they tear you into pieces'?"

"I'm John the potter's son. Some say I'm a pickpocket. But don't believe everything you hear."

"But this tearing to pieces…"

"Oh, that." Tiny John waved away the question. "He was right upset, he was. Losing a chunk of his finger and all." He paused to elaborately spit his mouth clean, then grinned. "I begged him not to throw me into this cell. Told him these two"—Tiny John gestured at Thomas and William—"were unforgiving about some jewelry I'd lifted and that I was sure to be killed if he threw me in the same den."

Waleran scowled. "These two would kill you?"

"Of course not," Tiny John said in amazement at Waleran's stupidity. "But how else could I make sure the guard would put me among my friends?"

Waleran sighed.

Tiny John continued in the same cheery voice. "I'm here now, Thomas. Right at eventide as requested. 'Twas no easy task running slow enough for the soldiers to catch me. Especially with so many of my village friends trying to help me escape."

"Right at eventide as requested?" Waleran repeated. He looked to Thomas for help. "He wanted to be captured?"

Thomas casually scratched his ear. "I promised him he would be out tonight."

"Tonight? But you told me the escape is tomorrow!" Waleran blurted.

Thomas ignored that and placed both his hands on Tiny John's shoulders. "The villagers expect an angel?"

"Some believe. Some don't. But all wait for tonight."

"Angel?" Waleran interjected. "Tonight?"

Thomas did not remove his gaze from Tiny John's face. "And Katherine has spread word among the villagers?"

"They wait for angels," Tiny John said. "No other legend could prepare them so."

"Angels?" Waleran almost stamped the ground in frustration.

Thomas removed his hands from the boy's shoulders. "Well done, Tiny John." Then he faced Waleran. "Yes. Angels. Surely, as one born in Magnus, you recall the legend?"

Waleran opened his mouth and snapped it shut.

William was quick to notice. "Thomas," he said sharply, "what is it you know about this man?"

Waleran edged away from them both.

Thomas replied with a question. "Do you not think it strange that one who claims to have been in this cell ten years remains so strong and healthy?"

"The rats," Waleran said quickly. "They provide nourishment when I tire of their friendship."

"Draw your sword, please, William," Thomas continued in a calm tone. "If this man opens his mouth to speak again, remove his head. The guards must not hear him shout for help."

As a fighting man, William had magical quickness. Almost instantly, Waleran faced the prick of a sword blade pushing against the soft skin of his throat.

"Explain," William told Thomas in a quiet voice. "I do not care to threaten innocent men."

"Waleran is a spy," Thomas said. "Each night, as we lay in drugged sleep, he leaves the cell and reports to his master."

"Drugged sleep?"

"Drugged sleep," Thomas repeated. He thought of the mornings he had licked his dry lips and stared at the ceiling. "I believe it is a potion placed into our water each night at supper."

"That explains why you asked me not to drink tonight."

Thomas nodded. "Also, these fetters. I began to wonder why we were not manacled to the walls, as is custom. But Waleran needed to have freedom of movement. We would have suspected too much if we were bound in iron and he were not. Ask him if he was placed in this cell hours before our arrival, or years as he claimed."

William added pressure to the sword point. "Is the accusation true? Are you a spy?"

Waleran did not reply.

"Answer enough." William held his sword steady and gazed thoughtfully at Waleran. "The foul taste as I woke. The dreamless nights. How I did not suspect…"

"It took me some time too," Thomas said. He glanced at the ceiling as if thanking the drips of water that had confirmed his suspicion after reading the note from Katherine. "Do your arms tire, William?"

"Of holding a sword to this scum's throat? I think not."

"Please. Let me sit," Waleran suggested nervously. His Adam's apple bobbed against the sword point. "If the sword slips…"

William nodded. "Sit then. But so much as draw a deep breath to shout for help and you shall be dead."

Waleran burrowed into the straw.

William did not remove his eyes from Waleran's face. "Thomas, Tiny John said we would escape tonight. Yet nearly a week ago…"

"I announced it would happen tomorrow. For the same reason I wanted him to see that you had a sword. If the guards searched for it, that would tell us he was a spy, and he wouldn't allow that, so I knew that secret would be safe. I wanted him to think we trusted him completely so we could plan in safety for escape at a different time."

"Does the lord of Magnus believe we escape tomorrow?" William asked with deceptive calm. His eyes had not wavered from Waleran's face.

"You expect me to reply?"

William pushed slightly harder on the sword blade and Waleran gasped. "These are your choices," William said. "You answer me and merely risk punishment from him. Or you refuse to answer me at the certainty of immediate death. After all, I stand to lose nothing by slaying you."

"Yes," came the quick reply. "At night while you sleep, I tell the guards what I know about you." He dropped his head. "Except for the sword. As Thomas said, if they took it from you, then you'd know I was the one who told."

"Where," Thomas asked, "will we find Richard Mewburn, the lord of Magnus, tonight?"

Waleran smiled. "If I tell you that, I am no longer merely risking punishment. Should you actually escape and reach him, he will know you could only have discovered that knowledge from one source. And if you don't escape—much more likely—then you don't need the knowledge anyway."

"Why were you placed here as a spy?" William asked. "Why would Richard Mewburn think Thomas and I were important enough to need watching in this cell? I came in as a beggar and Thomas as—"

"And why were you placed here ahead of our arrest?" Thomas asked.

The answer came as Thomas feared.

"Your arrival—and mission—was expected."

The old man at the gallows! There was no other possible way for anyone in Magnus to know! Thomas almost swayed as he fought the rush of adrenaline that swept him.

"Tell me who foretold our arrival!" he said in a voice coarsened by urgency. "And where he is now!"

Waleran shrugged and continued his eerie smile. "I am simply a spy. I only know there are many dark secrets in Magnus."

William glowered. "Explain yourself."

"That is all I will reveal. Death itself is a more attractive alternative."

Thomas felt chilled. Again, the dark secrets of Magnus. Then he clamped his jaw. The only magic in any kingdom was the power held by the lords. And if the moor winds continued to blow, morning would find him holding that power.

"Ignore his blathering," Thomas said as he focused on the task ahead. "William, there is much I need to tell you before we leave this cell tonight."

Waleran giggled. "You persist in believing you might leave?"

Thomas nodded at Tiny John, who grinned brightly from a dirt-smudged face and pulled from his coat a large key.

"Pickpockets do have their uses," Thomas said.

William frowned. "Any moment the guard will discover it missing and return."

"Not likely," Thomas said. "Just as Katherine instructed, Tiny John lifted it three days ago when the guard strolled through the marketplace. Katherine waited at the candle shop, then made a wax impression of it so that Tiny John could return the key within minutes. What you now see is a duplicate."

William began to grin as widely as Tiny John, then stopped abruptly. "How do you propose we silence this spy? We have no rope. No gag. As soon as I drop this sword, he'll call for help."

Thomas smiled. "He should sleep soon. I switched cups during supper. Waleran drank the drugged water intended for me."

"Not good enough," William said. "I can't keep my sword at his throat until then. And all it's going to take is one good shout. Especially now that he knows our intentions."

"No," Waleran croaked. "I promise; I want to live."

"Then you'll thank me for this," William said. He smashed the side of Waleran's head with his right elbow, and the man collapsed.

TWENTY-SIX

The beginning of their escape was as simple as letting Tiny John reach between the bars of the door with his slender arm and use the key on the lock.

"Wait," William said. He stepped back to Waleran and pinched one of the man's eyelids. Waleran didn't so much as flinch.

"We've got time then before he shouts for help," William said. "Let's move."

They began to creep down the hallway, guided by light from the candles on the walls. They encountered the first guard within ten heartbeats of easing themselves from the dungeon cell. Startled, the guard stepped backward and placed a hand on the hilt of his sword.

William was faster. Much faster.

Before the guard could flinch, William's sword point pinned his chest against the wall. The guard dropped his hand and waited.

"Run him through!" Tiny John urged.

"Spare his life," Thomas said in voice that allowed no argument.

"Thomas, I'm not fond of killing people. Believe me. Yet this man has been trained to do the same to us. At the very least, he will sound the alarm."

Even in the yellow light cast by the candles, the man's fear was obvious in the sweat that rolled down his face.

"You have children?" Thomas asked.

The guard nodded.

"Spare him," Thomas repeated. "I would wish a fatherless life on no one."

William shrugged. Then in a swift motion, he crashed his free fist into the guard's jaw. The guard groaned once, then sagged.

"We'll drag him back into our cell," Thomas instructed. Then he spoke to Tiny John through a smile that robbed his words of rebuke. "This isn't a game, you scamp. Would *you* care to have a sword through your chest?"

Tiny John squinted in thought. "Perhaps not."

Within moments, they left the guard as motionless as a sack of apples beside the snoring Waleran. Ten minutes later, they reached, undetected, the cool night air and the low murmur of a village settling at the end of an evening.

Thomas smiled at the wind that tugged at his hair.

In the early evening darkness outside the castle walls, Thomas forced away his fear. Planning in the idle hours, he told himself, was much too easy. In grand thoughts and wonderful schemes, you never considered the terror of avoiding guards on the battlements and dropping down by rope into a lake filled with black water. He shivered in his dampness.

Katherine must be here. Or all is lost.

William must rally the village people. Or all is lost.

The winds must hold. Or all is lost.

"Cast not your thoughts toward the fears," Sarah's patient voice echoed in his memory, *"but focus on your wishes."*

Thomas grinned at the moonlight. *Focus on your wishes.*

"I want to fly like an angel," he whispered. "Wind, carry me high and far."

As if reading his mind, the wind grew. But with it, so did the coldness of his wet clothing.

Five more minutes, he told himself. *If Katherine doesn't appear within five minutes, then I'll call out.*

He counted to mark time as he walked. *"The winds blow from the north,"* she had said. *"Once you reach the open moors, mark the highest point of the hills against the horizon and move toward it. I shall appear."*

With no warning, she did.

"You have retrieved your bundle?" she whispered.

"Yes. Undisturbed."

"Then wrap this around you."

Thomas slipped into a rough wool blanket.

"I've also brought you dry clothing," she said.

Without thinking, Thomas drew her into the blanket, hugged her, and lightly kissed the bandage at her forehead. It surprised him as much as her, and she pulled back awkwardly.

"I'm sorry," he said. "It's just that—"

"Please, dress quickly. Time is short."

Thomas removed his shirt and trousers with numbed fingers. The wind cut his bare skin, but within moments he was fully dressed. Immediately, his skin began to glow with renewed warmth.

"When I am lord," he promised, "you shall have your heart's desire."

"You do not know my heart's desire," she whispered softly.

Thomas did not reply. He was searching the bundle, quickly pulling out sheets and wooden rods. The moonlight aided him.

"I did this as a young child to pass time after my nurse died," Thomas spoke as he worked. This far from the castle walls—several hundred yards—there was no danger in being overheard by night watchmen. "But I confess it was on a smaller scale." He tied two rods together at one end, then propped and tied a cross member halfway down, so that the large frame formed an *A*. "However, I have no fear of this failing." He did, of course. "In a strange land, far, far away, it is a custom for men to build one of these to test the gods for omens before setting sail on a voyage."

"How is it you know these things?" Katherine stood beside him, handing him string and knives and wax as requested.

I will not mention the books, only what I learned as a child.

"You must vow to tell no person." Thomas waited until she nodded. "What I am building comes from the land known as Cathay."

"Cathay! That is at the end of the world!"

Thomas nodded. His hands remained in constant motion. He tested the frame. Satisfied, he moved it to a sheet of cloth spread flat across the grass.

"It is a land with many marvels," he said as if he had not paused. "The people there know much of science and medicine. I expect they would be called wizards here."

"'Tis wondrous strange," Katherine breathed.

Thomas nodded, thinking of his greatest possessions, the books hidden at the abbey. "Their secrets enabled me to win the services of a knight. And now, through the legend of Magnus, a kingdom." He knelt beside the frame. "Needle and thread."

Instantly, she placed it in his hands. He began to sew the sheet to the frame. For the next hour, he concentrated on his task and did not speak.

In equal silence, Katherine placed more thread in his hands as required. The moonlight, bright enough to cast shadows across their work, hastened their task.

Finally, Thomas stood and arched his back to relieve the strain. He took the structure and set it upright. The wind nearly snatched it from his hands, and he dropped it again. Satisfied, he surveyed it where it lay on the ground. As wide as a cart and as high as a doorway.

There still remained the sewing of bonds that would attach him to the structure. And after that, the flight.

Katherine interrupted his thoughts. Her voice quavered. "You are certain the men of Cathay used such a thing?"

Thomas was glad to speak of what he knew from the books. It took his thoughts from his fears.

"There is a man from Italy named Marco Polo," he began. "He spent nearly twenty years living among the people of Cathay." Thomas remembered how he had savored every word of the books, how each page helped ease the pain of daily living at the abbey. "This Marco Polo recorded many things. Among them, the custom of sending a man aloft in the winds before a ship sailed from shore. If the man flew, the voyage would be safe. If the man did not, the voyage was delayed."

Katherine spoke quickly. "There were times it did not stay in the air?"

"Tonight will not be one of them," Thomas vowed. "Too much has happened to bring me this far."

"Then it is God's will that you triumph," Katherine replied.

For the first time since Sarah's death, Thomas permitted a crack in his determined wall of disbelief.

"If that is indeed truth, begin a prayer," he said. "Begin it from both of us."

The winds held steady.

Thomas ignored the cold as he raced to final readiness. He tied leather shoulder straps to the cross members of the structure and another wide leather band that would secure his legs.

Do not think of failure.

He drove a peg into the ground with the hammer Katherine had smuggled out earlier.

My death here would be of no matter. Should I fail, life will not be important to me. I will never have a chance like this again.

To the peg, he attached one end of a roll of twine, the last object from his bundle.

Do not think of failure.

The other end of twine he tied to a belt of leather around his waist. Between both ends, the remaining twine was rolled neatly on a large spool. Small knots every three feet thickened the twine.

Will the knight be inside waiting with the new army?

Thomas looped the handles of a small, heavy bag around his neck. The cords of the bag bit fiercely into his skin and brought water to his eyes.

Do not think of failure.

Finally, he slipped his hands into crudely sewn gloves of heavy leather.

Will the winds be strong enough? Katherine, pray hard for me.

"I will lie down on this," he said. "Attach the straps around my shoulders. That will leave me movement with my arms. When I am ready, please help me to my feet. Then stand aside. The wind should do the rest."

Moving onto his back relieved some of the pressure of the cords around his neck. Katherine helped him fasten the straps securely, and Thomas took a deep breath.

You have dreamed long enough of this moment. Wait no longer.

"I am ready."

Katherine reached for his outstretched hand. She braced herself, then heaved backward. Thomas lurched to his feet with the huge structure on his back.

"Wings of an angel," Katherine breathed in awe.

Twenty-Seven

The wind snatched at Thomas. He grabbed the twine where it was secured to the peg. It took all his strength to hold to the ground.

"Thomas!" Katherine pointed behind him at the castle. "Soldiers! At the gate!"

He glanced over. Four of them, running hard toward them. But he was helpless to do anything. He was bound to a kite that was at the mercy of the wind, about to drive him toward a brutally high castle wall, two hundred carefully paced steps away. Would that distance give him time to gain the height to soar over it?

The wind screamed at the sail on his back.

Soldiers.

"Run, Katherine!" he shouted. "Away from the castle. Rejoin me tomorrow!"

"Go! God be with you!" She pushed him, and a gust of wind pulled the twine through his hands.

Airborne!

In the next frenzied seconds, Thomas could not afford to worry about the approaching soldiers. The kite picked up momentum so quickly that twine sang through his fingers. Even through heavy leather gloves, Thomas felt the heat.

The moon cast his shadow on the ground, and from his height, it appeared like a huge darting bat. The soldiers below him shouted and pointed upward.

Thomas dismissed any joy in this flight. He forced the soldiers from his mind. Instead, he concentrated sharply on counting each knot. His mind became a blur of numbers. He reached one hundred once, then began over. At eighty again, he clutched hard and the kite swooped upward even more sharply. His fingers froze.

Katherine!

The same moon that cut such clear black shadows also showed too clearly that the soldiers had reached her.

Why hasn't she fled?

Thomas understood immediately. She protected the peg! Once the soldiers reached it, a single slash of a sword would sever Thomas from the ground. She knew it.

"Run!" he screamed again. But his words were lost to the wind.

The knight had been watching from the nearest trees.

As the soldiers rushed toward Katherine, he stepped out and closed the distance. His blood surged with the familiar adrenaline of battle. This is what he'd been born to do. Not to play the games of deceit that had been so necessary until now.

He was a fighter, a man of action.

He roared with savage joy, and the sound was enough to distract the approaching soldiers but not enough to slow them down.

William took a stand in front of Katherine.

"Watch Thomas," he said to her. "These are mine."

The four soldiers should have separated more quickly, but they were overconfident. Instead of allowing them to take the battle to him as they probably expected, William attacked, his sword clanging hard against the first soldier's sword, snapping it in half.

With a startled cry, the man dropped the hilt and fled.

Down to three.

It would be tricky, and William had no illusions. Three against one were easy odds if it was a knight against three peasants, but these men were equally armed and well trained. Without doubt, they wore chain mail as protection. William did not. It would give him an advantage of sorts, for the weight of the chain mail would make them slower and tire them faster.

One of the soldiers advanced, showing a degree of swordsmanship in his stance. The other two spread apart to begin to form a triangle.

Without Katherine to protect, the battle would have been easier, for William could have slashed his way out of the triangle.

Already he was breathing heavily. He expected this and hoped the time in the jail cell had not robbed him of too much of his strength.

A movement came from the side. William whirled and parried, able to get his sword up in time, but the blow was still jarring. These men were equal to him in fighting ability.

He began to realize he'd pay with his life to keep Thomas safe in the air.

Then one of the soldiers yelped and brought his hand to his face.

"Got more where that came from," Tiny John yelled with glee. Another rock found its target on another soldier's face. Not enough damage to put either of them down, but John's sling provided a satisfying distraction for the knight. He pressed in on one of the soldiers, dropped to his non-sword hand, and kicked outward, feeling the impact of the bottom of his foot against the man's groin. No chain mail there.

The man fell to his knees as William bounced to his feet again, whirling his sword in a wide arc of protection.

"Here I am," Tiny John shouted. "Can't you catch a boy?"

He fired another rock, drawing another oath of anger.

With a flurry of swings, William drove the third soldier away, then found an open spot in the man's defenses. He swung for the man's head, and at the last second gave a twist of the wrist, smacking him solidly with the flat of his blade. The man dropped.

That left one soldier.

William squared his body to the man. Now the odds were favorable.

Except the man who fallen to his knees reached out with a hand and tripped him. William fell sideways, trying to turn to stay facing his final opponent. On his own knees, he parried twice, thrice. But he felt the sword get knocked out of his hands as he parried the fourth blow. With the leverage that came with standing, his opponent had much more power.

The soldier stood over him and placed the tip of his sword against William's chest, preparing to shove it forward.

"Is he over the castle walls?" William asked.

"You'll not distract me," the soldier said, keeping his focus on William.

But William had distracted the soldier. Tiny John had pocketed his sling and found the broken sword dropped by the first solider. The boy was advancing.

It was only a stub of a sword, with about two feet of the original four-foot blade.

But enough.

Tiny John took a mighty swipe and swung the blade's edge across the soldier's buttocks.

"Take that!" the boy shouted.

William took advantage of his opponent's shock, spun sideways, found his own sword, and leapt to his feet.

But there was no fight left in the last soldier. Tiny John's mighty swipe had undoubtedly cut deeply into the man's buttocks, and he was clutching the wound, attempting to staunch the blood loss.

"And you take that!" Tiny John kicked the groaning soldier who had reached out to trip William.

Tiny John dropped his broken sword and picked up the one that had fallen from the soldier who had taken the swipe across the buttocks. He struggled with the weight but managed to lift it.

"Give me that," William said. "Before you hurt someone with it."

"But you're supposed to do that with a sword."

"Not anymore," William said. "This battle is over."

Thomas ached to try to look behind him. Yet he needed all his attention to be on what was ahead. How far from the castle walls? He only knew he was not high enough yet to get over the rough stone.

He willed his fingers to release the cord. Eighty-one. Eighty-two. Eighty-three.

A scream pierced the darkness.

Concentrate!

At ninety-nine, he stopped the unraveling by swiftly lashing the twine around his wrist in two loops. It felt as if the sudden stop tore his

hand loose. With his other hand, he fumbled with the sack at his neck
and pulled free a grappling hook. It, too, was attached to twine, and
Thomas dropped it like an anchor, knowing there was ample cord remaining attached to the sack around his neck.

Without the extra weight of the grapple, the kite bobbed upward,
high enough to clear the castle wall.

At the same time, the tremendous pressure on his lashed wrist
ceased.

The rope's been cut! Katherine!

"Please, God. Be with us now!" Thomas cried into the black wind,
startled that at the moment of his greatest terror, he called out to a deity
he did not want to acknowledge.

The grappling hook hit the surface of the drawbridge and bounced
as the wind took the kite. Savagely, with all the anger he wanted to di-
rect at the soldiers who had made Katherine scream, Thomas wrapped
his fingers around the twine that unraveled from the sack around his
neck. The grapple hopped upward again and clacked against the wall
of the gate before spinning away.

By then, Thomas was over the walls and in sight of anyone within
Magnus. A great shout rose to meet him. William *had* gathered the
army!

Clank. The grapple bounced against the lower part of the walls.
Thomas held his breath.

The kite tore upward so quickly that barely any wall remained between the grapple and the night sky. If it did not catch, the wings of an
angel would carry Thomas far, far away from Magnus. Without
Thomas, William's army would scurry homeward. Never would Magnus be freed from…

Thud.

Twine spun through his gloves at the sudden lurch of kite against wind as the grapple dug into the top of the castle wall.

The shouts of people below him grew louder.

Thomas still did not dare look downward. He fought the twine to a standstill, then looped it around his waist. Then, and only then, did he survey Magnus.

The kite hung as high as the highest tower. Suspended as it was against the moon, people gathered below could only see the outspread wings of white. They roared, "Delivered on the wings of an angel, he shall free us from oppression! Delivered on the wings of an angel, he shall free us from oppression!"

Thomas nearly wept with relief. He pulled his crude gloves free and tucked them among the remaining twine in the sack around his neck.

"Delivered on the wings of an angel, he shall free us from oppression!"

Thomas could see the villagers armed with hoes and pitchforks, protected by rough shields of tabletops and helmets of pots. As they shouted, they pumped their hands upward in defiance.

That was the secret to conquering Magnus. Not to find a way to bring an army into it, but to form one from the people already inside. One knight to lead them. One angel to inspire them.

"Delivered on the wings of an angel, he shall free us from oppression!"

The roar of their noise filled the sky. There were enough people to pack the market space and spill into the alleys. Thomas could see no soldiers foolish enough to approach the roiling crowd.

"Delivered on the wings of an angel, he shall free us from oppression!"

Thomas blinked away tears of an emotion he could not understand.

"Delivered on the wings of an angel, he shall free us from oppression!"

TWENTY-EIGHT

I t was time to return to earth.

Thomas found the knife in his inner shirt. He twisted against the shoulder straps and reached behind him.

Slash. He tore open a slit in the white cloth. Wind whistled through and the kite sagged downward. Another slash. Slowly, the kite began to drop foot by foot as its resistance to the wind lessened.

As Thomas neared the ground, be began to loosen the straps around his shoulders and his legs. Then, just before the kite could die completely, he released himself and cut through the twine. The kite bobbed upward as Thomas fell. He rolled with the impact and stood immediately.

The crowd, with William at the front and Tiny John at his side, advanced in a wave toward him.

"Delivered on the wings of an angel, he shall free us from oppression!"

Thomas held up his right hand. Instant silence at the front of the crowd. The silence rolled backward as each wave of villagers took its cue from the wave in front. Within a minute, it was quiet enough for Thomas to hear his own thudding heart.

What do I say?

William rescued him.

"Thomas!" he called. "Thomas of Magnus!"

In a great chant, the crowd took up those words. "Thomas of Magnus. Thomas of Magnus." Like thunder, his name rolled inside the castle walls.

Thomas was not lord yet. Richard Mewburn would not have simply fled into the hills at the sight of an angel. The battle was not over.

Then Thomas remembered. *Katherine!*

He held up his hand again. Again, the silence sifted backward.

"William," Thomas cried, "the gate is open and half the soldiers are outside. If you take the gate now, they will be unable to return."

William understood immediately. The army was divided already. It took little urging for him to gather a hundred men.

"Wait," Thomas cried again. "Find Katherine."

The knight nodded and moved forward. One hundred angry men followed.

Thomas closed his eyes briefly. What had he seen from his perch in the sky? Soldiers scurrying to their last retreat, the keep itself, four stories tall and unassailable.

Tonight, these villagers were an army, unified by emotion and hope. The remaining soldiers would not fight. They knew, as did Thomas, that tomorrow or the day after these fierce emotions would fade. When that happened, the villagers would no longer be a solid army, prepared to die in a fight for freedom. Then, once again, a handful of trained fighters would be able to conquer and dominate seven hundred people.

The battle must be won tonight!

Thomas thought hard. Then it struck him.

He cast his eyes toward the keep. Unlike the castle walls, it had not been designed for soldiers to fight downward from above. The solution, once it hit him, was obvious.

"Good people of Magnus!"

Whatever shuffling of impatience there was in the crowd stopped immediately.

"Enough blood has been shed within these walls. Enough cruel oppression. Enough pain and bitterness. Tomorrow's dawn brings a new age in Magnus!"

The roar began. "Delivered on the wings of an angel, he shall free us from oppression!"

Thomas held up his hand again. "Our captors, now captive, shall be treated with kindness!"

To this, there was low grumbling.

"Do you not remember the pain inflicted on you?" Thomas shouted. "It is double the sin, knowing full well the pain, to inflict it in return."

Immediate silence, then murmurings of agreement. "We have a wise and kind ruler!" a voice yelled from the middle of the mob.

"Wise and kind! Wise and kind!"

Again, Thomas requested silence. "Furthermore," he shouted, "we shall not inflict injury upon ourselves by attempting to storm the keep."

A hum of questions reached him.

"Instead," Thomas shouted, "we shall wait until the remaining army surrenders." Before he could be interrupted again, Thomas picked a large man from the front of the crowd. "You, my good man, gather two hundred. Arm yourselves with spades and shovels and meet me in front of the keep." He pointed at another. "You, gather fifty men and all the tar and kindling in the village."

With that, Thomas turned and strode toward the keep. He did not have to look behind him to know hundreds followed in a large milling crowd.

A quarter of an hour later, the two smaller groups joined Thomas and the main crowd in front of the keep. During that time, not one soldier had even ventured to stick his head outside a casement of the keep.

With the arrival of all the village's men, Thomas quickly began to outline his plan. The men grasped it immediately. Many grinned in appreciation.

William approached him with long strides. "Our men have barricaded the remaining soldiers outside the walls," he said with a grim furrow across his forehead. "Yet there is no sign of the girl Katherine. Alive or dead."

Thomas beat his side once with his right fist. *This is no time to show pain or mourning,* he told himself. He made his face expressionless under the bright lights of hundreds of torches.

"We cannot forsake the kingdom for one person," he told William. "When this battle is complete, I will search for her."

It took until noon the next day—and three shifts of one hundred men each—to complete Thomas's plan for bloodless warfare. When they were finished, the keep had effectively been isolated from the rest of the village within the castle walls.

The men had dug a shallow moat around it, throwing the dirt to the village side as a barricade. Thomas then had the moat filled with tar and pitch and kindling. Standing guard every twelve paces were men armed with torches. There was no shortage of volunteers for the four-hour shifts.

After the final barrel of pitch had oozed into the moat, Thomas called loudly up at the keep, "Who wishes to speak to the new lord of Magnus?"

All of the villagers stood gathered behind Thomas. Tomorrow, or the day after, they might resume normal life. Today, however, was a day to behold. A new lord was about to dictate terms of surrender to the old lord.

A single face appeared in a casement on the third floor. "I am the captain."

Thomas said, "Not a single soldier shall die. But we will not provide food or water. You may surrender when you wish. Be warned, however, that should you decide to fight, the moat will impede any battle rush upon the village. And as you struggle to cross the pitch, it shall be set aflame!"

"We have heard that you deal with fairness," the captain replied.

Thomas frowned in puzzlement.

"One of our men thanks you for his life," the captain explained.

The prison guard they had left with Waleran. *And what has become of that spy?*

"When you are prepared to surrender," Thomas instructed, "one of your men must deliver all your weapons to the edge of the moat. Then, and only then, will we build you a bridge to safety." Thomas paused. "Your lord will also be granted his life upon surrender."

The captain said, "That will not be necessary. Nor will a prolonged siege."

"What is that you say?"

"There is a tunnel that leads to the lake. The former lord of Magnus fled with two others during the night. We wish to surrender immediately."

TWENTY-NINE

F are thee well, Thomas."

"I wish that it were not this way," Thomas replied to William.

The knight smiled his ironic half smile. Beside him, his horse, a great roan stallion from the stables of Magnus, danced and shook its mane with impatience.

"Thomas," William said, "I have fulfilled my vow to you. Magnus is yours. All that remains is for you to pledge allegiance to the king, promise to pay your taxes, and offer your soldiers to him if needed. You aren't the first to have gained a castle by power, and no one will risk taking it from you if it is easier for him to let you keep it."

Thomas held his head high. He must fight the lump in his throat. "You still dispense advice."

"Listen, lad," the knight growled. "None of us is ever too smart to throw away good advice."

Thomas squinted into the morning sun to blaze into his memory his last look at the knight. Not for the first time did he wonder about the scar on William's face. Or where he was going. Or from where he had arrived.

An early breeze gently flapped the knight's colors against the stallion. Behind them, at the other end of the narrow land bridge, lay the walls of Magnus. Ahead, the winding trail that would lead William into the moors.

"Then I thank you for all your good advice," Thomas said in a quiet voice. "Without it, I would have foundered."

Thomas knew too well the truth of his words. Within hours of forcing the soldiers to surrender, Thomas had discovered a position as lord meant much more than simply accepting tribute as he had naively dreamed. No, the lord of a manor or village was also administrator, sometimes judge, sometimes jailer.

William had first guided Thomas through the task of selecting his army from the soldiers. Those who swore loyalty remained. Those who didn't normally were skinned alive by flogging, or worse, if the lord chose. Thomas had not. He did not want any men pretending loyalty merely to escape death. As a result, most of the men had been eager to serve a new master.

Over the last two days, William had taken Thomas through his new tasks as lord. Thomas had grown more confident, and along with that, earned the confidence of the villagers. Had any of them doubted their new lord because of his youth, the doubts quickly disappeared.

Thomas truly was lord of Magnus.

As lord, he hid his grief from public view. Katherine had not been found. Nor had there been any trace of Isabelle.

Thomas's thoughts must have become obvious in those moments of farewell.

"You brood once more." William's voice interrupted his thoughts. "Perhaps the time is not ready for my departure."

Thomas forced a grin. "So that I must endure more of your nagging? I think not. Be on your way."

Before the moment could become awkward, William mounted his horse.

"I thank you for my life," William said with a salute. "You have your destiny. I have mine."

The drumming of the horse's hooves remained with Thomas all of that day.

One mile past the crest of the hill that overlooked the valley of Magnus, the knight reined his horse to a halt. He hobbled its front feet and let it find grass among the heather and gorse.

Earlier it had been warm, but weather changed quickly on the moors, even as spring approached summer. The scattered clouds above him were low, heavy at the bottom with angry gray, and moved over the hills in a growing wind he felt more keenly outside the protective walls of Magnus. It would not be a good day for travel.

Still he waited.

Here, against the horizon, he would be in plain view. And here, against the horizon, none would be able to approach him without being equally plain to see.

Hawkwood did not keep the knight waiting long enough to shiver. William saw him first as a small black figure stepping out from the trees below, a figure that grew quickly as Hawkwood covered ground with long, vigorous strides.

"My friend," the knight called, "you wear the guise of an old man but move as a puppy. Merlin himself would find it a performance sadly lacking."

Hawkwood shook his head and raised his voice to be heard above the moor winds. "Merlin himself would rest beside a fire when the cold begins to move across the hills. If I walked like an old man, I would soon feel like one."

"I feel like one now," William said. "It was no easy task to leave the young lord."

"He does inspire affection," Hawkwood agreed. "Katherine, too, does not want to believe he serves a different cause."

"Katherine. She is well?" The knight could not keep sharp anxiety from his voice. "All that Gervaise could relay was that she had escaped the soldiers."

Hawkwood nodded. "She suffered one blow, but the bandages softened the club's impact, and she has rested well. It helped that I was able to run horses through the midst of them, and the exploding powder from Cathay accomplished the rest."

William relaxed. "And now?"

"Now we have the luxury of time and privacy for her to be taught in our ways."

"The luxury of time? You don't fear the fate of Magnus?"

"Always," Hawkwood said. The wind plucked at his hood, and he threw it back to expose his silver hair. "But I fear it will be unwise to force whatever happens next. It will serve us better to wait and watch. Gervaise, of course, is there, and I hope to continue to find ways to wander freely throughout Magnus when necessary. Over twenty years have passed. Another few months will not hurt."

"No? If Thomas is not one of theirs, they will double their efforts. Who will protect him from an enemy he cannot see?"

Hawkwood leaned forward, both hands on the head of his cane. "If he is not one of theirs, they will assume he is ours and play the waiting game too. Besides, if they truly wanted him dead, there is naught we could do. As you well know, dealing death is too simple. Poison, an asp beneath his bed covers, a dart from one of the passageways."

"Your task is to wait and watch," the knight said heavily, "while I return to exile to rely on messages that take months to receive. I do not know which is the more difficult burden."

THIRTY

Three days later at sunrise, two soldiers escorted Isabelle into the keep of the castle.

"Thomas," she said with a bow.

"Isabelle," Thomas replied softly. He did not rise from his large chair in the front hall despite his flood of joy.

She stood in front of him, looking around with admiration. Tapestries hung on the walls. The fireplace crackled, for even in the summer, early mornings were cool. Two soldiers guarded the entrance, stiffly unmoving. Soon enough, as William had warned, Thomas would have to deal with officialdom outside of the territory of Magnus, but for now, it seemed the castle was his.

Seeing Isabelle, he wanted to weep with joy. Instead, he dismissed the soldiers. Too much, he was conscious of the dignity required as the man who had bloodlessly conquered the army of Magnus.

When they were alone, he whispered her name again. "Isabelle."

She lowered her head, looked upward, and said shyly, "Yes, Thomas."

He wanted to throw himself into her arms. He knew, watching her, that she would embrace him gladly in return.

"Isabelle," he started again. Although he could will himself to remain in his chair, he could not keep the hushed wonder from his tone.

"Your return is a miracle. Yet I am flooded with questions. Where have you been? How is it you prospered while away?"

She straightened her shoulders and looked him directly in the eyes. "There is much to tell. Will you listen, lord?"

"Gladly."

Her smile—a promise and a reward in one—drew from him a silent inward gasp. He managed to keep his face motionless. *She is worth as much as a kingdom.*

"I, like you, am an orphan, from a village far south of here. My parents perished in a fire when I was a baby. I am told the villagers did not think it worth their while to preserve me. But a lonely old woman, one who was truly mute and deaf, defeated them. She fought for me. The villagers, who suspected she was a witch, dared not disagree, and so she raised me. She died when I was ten. With her gone, the villagers were free to chase me away."

Thomas nodded. His heart ached for her. *She is an outcast too.*

"Because the old lady could not hear, I learned early to speak with my hands. And when I was forced to travel from village to village, seeking food and shelter, I soon discovered the advantages of posing as mute and deaf. It earned pity. Also, I learned not to trust, and being mute and deaf put me behind walls that no person could break." Isabelle faltered and looked down at her hands. "Not even you wanted me. You saved us all from death by hanging, but you only wanted the knight."

"That is no longer true," he said quickly and with some guilt.

"When you were arrested and before I returned to visit you in prison," she began again, "I fled Magnus. After three days of travel, I reached the dales near the town of York. I had not eaten. I had barely slept. I threw myself at the mercy of the first passing carriage. The lady inside took pity. She fed and clothed me and arranged for me to work as a maid in her kitchen. When word reached me of the fall of Magnus I returned. My heart could not rest until it discovered the answer."

"Answer?"

She moved forward to where he was sitting and grabbed his hands and tightened her grip. "Yes. Answer. Did I belong to you? Or had I been fooling myself about your glances?"

"I am the only fool," Thomas said gallantly. "Not to have searched the world for you."

She did not hesitate. She threw her arms around him. Thomas felt her warm skin on his neck and—pressed tight as she was—the cool circle of her medallion.

"Take them with you." The old man's words at the hanging. *"It will guarantee you a safe journey to Magnus."*

Even as Thomas held her, his mind raced with thoughts and questions.

Slowly, ever so slowly, he released her.

"You must answer me these further questions," Thomas said in a pained voice. "Who are you? And who placed you among us? Was it the old man at the gallows?"

"I—I do not understand."

"Yes," he said. "I believe you do."

He waited for her to speak. The silence stretched. Still he waited and said nothing.

Her voice broke upon the words. "How is it you know?"

Thomas sighed. A tiny hope had flickered that he was wrong, that he could still trust her.

"Your medallion," he said. "What a blunder to leave it around your neck upon your return."

She clutched it automatically.

"Do not fear," Thomas said heavily. "I have seen it already, the day Tiny John lifted it from you on the moors. The strange symbol upon it matches the symbol engraved that I've been told by elders among the village is a Druid symbol. There is more to you than what appears. I want to know what it is."

Isabelle shivered and hugged herself.

"Moreover," Thomas continued, "there was the soldiers' attack outside the walls of Magnus the night I was delivered on 'the wings of an angel.' How did they know to venture outside the walls? I had not been followed. No sentry could have seen me or Katherine. You and the knight and Tiny John were the only ones who knew I had hidden my bundle outside the castle walls."

Isabelle turned to face him.

"And our arrest," Thomas said. "It could not have been a coincidence. Or the fact that a spy had already been planted in the dungeon ahead of us. The knowledge of our presence in Magnus could only have come from you, the person who disappeared our first morning here to return with a few bowls of porridge to explain your absence."

Isabelle nodded.

The implications staggered Thomas. Isabelle's nearness had been planned before the hanging and the rescue of William. Again, it circled back to the old man and his knowledge at the gallows!

"Why? How?" Thomas said, almost quiet with despair. "My plans to conquer Magnus were a dream, kept only to myself. How did the lord know—"

"Why?" she said calmly. "Duty. I am Lord Richard Mewburn's daughter."

"Daughter! You were one of the three figures to escape the night of my conquering!" Thomas stopped, puzzled. "No one recognized you when you arrived with us."

"Do you think the lord of Magnus would dare let his daughter wander the streets among a people who hated him? No one recognized me because I spent so little time among them."

Thomas shook his head. "And duty dictated you return and pretend love for me?"

She nodded.

"How were you to kill me?" Thomas asked with bitterness. "Poison as I drank to your health? A ladylike dagger thrust in my ribs during a long embrace?"

A half sob escaped Isabelle. "Those...those were my father's commands. I don't know if I could have fulfilled them."

Thomas shrugged, although at her admission the last pieces of his heart fell into a cold black void. "No matter. I cared little for you."

She blinked, stung.

"Go on," Thomas said with the same lack of tone. "From the beginning. At the gallows."

"It was arranged I would be on the gallows. My father feared a threat to his kingdom, and he did not believe the knight would die."

That was the greatest mystery. "How did your father know? Did he instruct the old man to appear at the gallows? Or is it reversed—did the old man instruct your father of my intentions?"

"Old man?" Isabelle stared at Thomas for long moments. Then she threw her head back in laughter. When she finished and found her breath again, she said, almost with disbelief, "You truly do not know."

Thomas gritted his teeth. "I truly do not know *what*?"

"I was not there because of you. You were not the threat my father feared. I was there because of the knight." Isabelle kept her voice flat. "My father sometimes used cruel methods to maintain his power. I did not approve or disapprove. I am told that when my father first overthrew the lord of Magnus…"

Thomas gritted his teeth again. Sarah's parents. His own grandparents.

"…he publicly branded each opposing soldier and knight and had them flogged to death. One escaped. The most loyal and most valiant fighter of them all."

She let those words hang until Thomas grasped the truth.

"William!"

"Yes. William. When my father received word William had returned to this land, he paid a great sum of money to have the sacred chalices stolen and placed among William's belongings."

"You were sent to the hanging to be a spy should he be rescued. How did your father know it would happen?"

"He guessed it might. The hangman had instructions to release me if the knight died on the gallows."

Thomas paced to the far side of the room. "Why? Why did he foresee a rescue?" Nothing could be more important than this.

"Thomas," she began, "there is a great circle of conspiracy. Much larger than you and I. My father, too, acted upon the commands of another. And there is much at stake."

"You are speaking in riddles."

"Because I know only what I have guessed after a lifetime in Magnus. Haven't you wondered why this castle is set so securely, so far away from the outer world? Why would anyone bother attacking a village here? Yet an impenetrable castle was founded. And by no less a wizard than Merlin."

The door exploded open.

Time fragmented before Thomas's eyes. Geoffrey the candle maker ran toward them with a short club extended, the guards on his heels. Thomas leapt forward, seeing Geoffrey's obvious target. But he was too late. Geoffrey swung the club, smashing Isabelle across the head.

She collapsed.

With lifted swords, the guards were almost upon Geoffrey, who began to swing the club at Thomas.

"No! Don't!" Thomas roared as he dodged Geoffrey's first wild swing. "He must not be killed!"

Too late again. Geoffrey fell into a limp huddle. His arm and hand scraped the floor in a last feeble twitch.

Thomas could only stare at the ring Geoffrey wore.

He finally rose in the horrified silence shared by both guards.

"My lord, we did not know—"

Thomas waved a weary hand to stop the soldier's voice.

Isabelle lay motionless, blood matting her hair. He bent and gently took the medallion from her neck. Then he matched it to the ring on Geoffrey's hand.

The image was identical.

THIRTY-ONE

Each dawn found Thomas on the eastern ramparts of the castle walls. The guards knew to respect his need for privacy; each morning the sentry for that part of the wall would retreat at the sight of his approach.

The wind had yet to rise on the moors. The cry of birds carried from far across the lake surrounding Magnus. The first rays of sunlight edged over the top of the eastern slope and began to reflect off the calm water. Behind Thomas, the town lay silent.

It was the time of day that he searched his own emptiness. He'd fulfilled the beginning of the vow he'd made to his mother. But he still felt the grief as strongly as if he had buried her the day before.

"What now?" he said to the morning. "I thought this would be the end, but why does it seem like only the beginning? Who are the Immortals? Where are they? What must I do next?"

The morning did not answer.

He could keep a brave and resolute face as the new lord of Magnus. Yet in the quiet times, he still keenly felt alone. Journeying here, he had a family of sorts. Now he was an orphan again. An orphan king. With too many questions unanswered.

There is so little that I know, Thomas thought.

Who was the old man who cast the sun into darkness and directed me here from the gallows?

Why did William help me and then depart? Why did he keep secret his role in first defending Magnus?

What conspiracy was Isabelle about to reveal before her death? Why did she and the candle maker share the same strange symbol?

And what fate has fallen upon Katherine?

There is so much I must do, Thomas thought.

The book of priceless knowledge must be brought safely to the castle.

Magnus must be prepared for the arrival of the Earl of York.

And I must not cease in searching—without the villagers' awareness—for the secrets of Magnus.

Thomas closed his eyes.

For a moment, Katherine's voice echoed in his mind. He kept his eyes closed, desperate for any comfort. What had she once said? *"You and I are threads, Thomas. We cannot see God's plan for us."*

Thomas opened his eyes. The sun had broken over the top of the faraway hill, spilling rays across the dips and swells of the land. Thomas smiled. *Oh, that there were a God with enough love and wisdom to watch over all our follies.*

He speculated with wonder on that thought for many long minutes. He thought of Katherine's braveness and conviction. He thought of his own confusion.

Suddenly, Thomas spun on his heels and marched from the ramparts.

He strode through the village streets and came to a small stone building near the center market square. There, he banged against the rough wooden door.

A strong voice answered, and the door opened to show an elderly man with gray hair combed straight back.

"My lord," he said without fear. "Come inside, please. We are graced with your presence."

They moved to the nave at the front of the church. Sunlight streamed through the eastern windows and cut sharp shadows across both their faces. In the man's eyes, Thomas saw nothing of the greed he had witnessed those many years at the abbey. It was enough to encourage him to speak.

Thomas smiled tightly. He had spent much time considering Katherine's strong faith. And he could not forget that during his worst moment in the air, he had cried out to the God he thought he did not believe in.

"Father," Thomas said. "I have questions for you."

FORTRESS OF MIST

Available February 2013

I n the tent of his army camp, Thomas woke to the scent of a trace of perfume and the softness of hair falling across his face.

This was no soldier. How had she—

He drew breath to challenge the intruder, but he felt a light finger across his lips, and a gentle shushing stopped him from speaking.

"Dress quickly, Thomas. Follow without protest," the voice then whispered.

Thomas saw only the darkness of silhouette in the dimness of the tent where she knelt beside him.

"Do not be afraid," the voice continued. "An old man wishes to see you. He asks if you remember the gallows."

Old man. Gallows. In a rush of memory as bright as daylight, Thomas felt himself at the gallows. The knight who might win Magnus with him was about to hang, and Thomas waited in front, intent on attempting a rescue through disguise and trickery. Then the arrival of an old man, one who identified Thomas behind the disguise and knew of his quest, one who commanded the sun into darkness, one who had never appeared again.

"As you wish," Thomas whispered in return, with as much dignity as he could muster, despite the sudden trembling in his stomach. No mystery—not even the terror of the strange symbol of Magnus—was more important to him than discovering the old man's identity.

The silhouette backed away slowly, beckoning Thomas with a single crooked finger. He rose quickly, wrapped his cloak around him, and shuffled into his shoes.

How had she avoided the sentries outside his tent?

Thomas pushed aside the tent of the flap and followed. Moonlight shown on both sentries sitting crookedly against the base of a nearby tree.

Asleep. It was within his rights as earl to have them executed.

"Forgive them," the voice whispered as if reading his mind. "Their suppers contained potions."

He strained to see the face of the silhouette in the light of the large pale moon. In response, she pulled the flaps of her hood across her face. The tall and slender figure led him slowly along a trail that avoided all tents and campsites.

Ghost-white snakes of mist hung heavy among the solitary trees of the moor valley.

It felt too much like a dream to Thomas. Still, he did not fear to follow. Only one person had knowledge of what had transpired in front of the gallows—the old man himself. Only he, then, could have sent the silhouette to his tent.

At the farthest edge of the camp, she stopped to turn and wait.

When Thomas arrived, she took his right hand and clasped it with her left.

"Who are you?" Thomas asked. "Show me your face."

"Hush, Thomas," she whispered.

"You know my name. You know my face. Yet you hide from me."

"Hush," she repeated.

"No," he said with determination. "Not a step farther will I take. The old man wishes to see me badly enough to drug my sentries, so he'll be angry if you do not succeed in your mission. Show me your face or I turn around."

She did not answer. Instead, she lifted her free hand slowly, pulled the hood from her face, and shook her hair loose to her shoulders.

Nothing in his life had prepared him for that moment.

The sudden ache of joy to see her face hit him like a blow. For a timeless moment, it took from him all breath.

It was not her beauty that brought him that joy, even though the curved shadows of her face would be forever seared in her mind. No. Thomas had learned not to trust appearances, that beauty indeed consisted of heart joining heart, not eyes to eyes. Isabelle, now in the dungeon, had used her exquisite features to deceive, while gentle Katherine—horribly burned and masked by bandages—had proven the true worth of friendship.

Thomas struggled for composure. He couldn't understand it, but he felt drawn deeper into the world, as if he had been long pledged for this very moment.

She stared back, as if knowing how he felt, yet, unlike him, fearless of what was passing between them.

"Your name," Thomas said. "What is your name?"

"I don't have a name."

"Everyone has a name."

"Everyone of this world," she answered. "What if I am nothing more than a spirit? A walking dream?"

"You toy with me. As if you already know me. Who are you?"

"Someone who wants to believe that you are one of us," she answered.

"One of you. A spirit? A walking dream?"

As answer, she took his hand, lifted it to her mouth, and kissed the back of his hand so gently he wondered if he had imagined her lips brushing against his skin.

She dropped his hand again. "I have already said too much. Follow me. The old man wishes to see you."

Abruptly, she turned and he had no choice but to follow as she picked faultless footsteps through ground soon darkened from the moon by the trees along stream of the valley.

They walked—it could have only been a heartbeat, he felt so distant from the movement of time—until reaching a hill which rose steeply into the black of the night.

An owl called.

She turned to the sound and walked directly into the side of the hill. As if parting the solid rock by magic, she slipped sideways into an invisible cleft between monstrous boulders. Thomas followed.

They stood completely surrounded by granite walls of a cave long hollowed smooth by eons of rainwater. The air seemed to press down upon him, and away from the light of the moon Thomas saw only velvet black.

He heard her return the owl's call, but before he could question the noise, a small spark appeared. His eyes adjusted to see an old man holding the small light of a torch that grew as the pitch caught fire.

Light gradually licked upward around them to reveal a bent old man wrapped in a shawl. Beyond deep wrinkles, Thomas could distinguish no features—the shadows leapt and danced eerie circles from beneath his chin.

"Greetings, Thomas of Magnus." The voice was a slow whisper.

"Congratulations on succeeding in your first task, the conquering of the castle."

"My first task? Who are you?"

"Such impatience. One who is Lord of Magnus would do well to temper his words among strangers."

"I will not apologize." Thomas filled with indignation. "Each day I am haunted by memory of you. Impossible that you should know my quest at the hanging. Impossible that the sun should fail that morning at your command."

The old man shrugged. "Impossible is often merely a perception. Surely by now you have been able to ascertain the darkness was no sorcery, but merely a trick of astronomy as the moon moves past the sun. Your books would inform a careful reader that such eclipses may be anticipated, or predicted, as some might say."

"You know of my books!"

That mystery gripped Thomas so tightly he could almost forget the presence of the other in the cave. The young woman.

The old man ignored the urgency in Thomas's words. "My message is the same as before. You must bring the winds of light into this age and resist the forces of darkness poised to take Magnus from you. Otherwise, it'll be little more than a fortress of mist. The assistance I may offer is little—the decisions to be made are yours."

Thomas clenched his fists and let out a frustrated blast of air. "You talk in circles. Tell me who you are. Tell me—in clear terms, man— what you want of me. And tell me the secret of Magnus."

The old man turned away from Thomas, disappearing and reappearing in the shadows of the cave.

"Druids, Thomas. Beware those barbarians from the isle, Thomas. They will attempt to conquer you through force. Or through bribery."

Yet another layer of cryptic answers. "Tell me how you knew of my quest that day at the hanging. Tell me how you know of the books. Tell me how you know of the barbarians."

"To tell you is to risk all."

Thomas pounded his thigh in anger. "The risk is shrouded and hidden from me! I am given a task that is unexplained, and with no reason to fulfill it beyond my vow. And then you imply it is but the first of more tasks. No more circles."

Even as he fought his own frustration, Thomas sensed sadness from the old man.

"The knowledge you already have is worth the world, Thomas. That is all I can say."

"No," Thomas pleaded. "Who belongs to the strange symbol of conspiracy? Is the Earl of York friend or enemy?"

The old man shook his head. "Thomas, very soon you will be offered a prize which seems far greater than the kingdom of Magnus."

The torch flared once before dying, and Thomas read deep concern in the old man's eyes.

From the sudden darkness came the old man's whispered words. "It is worth your soul to refuse."